I0611564

# Man Among the Missing

Alex Mitchell

Published by Alex Mitchell, 2023.

MAN AMONG THE MISSING

**First edition. October 13, 2023.**

Copyright © 2023 Alex Mitchell.

ISBN: 979-8891980105

Written by Alex Mitchell.

# Also by Alex Mitchell

# Chapter One

Mosses rushed into the Eastern Star Cleaners.

Marta was business waiting on an elderly lady that seemed confused about her change.

"Yes, ma'am, this is the correct amount."

"I guess I must have thought it cost less. Did you raise your prices?" The old woman asked in an accusatory tone.

Mosses looked shaken, and it was clear to Marta that he wanted to talk to her. Jacob, the other person that worked with them at the cleaners, noticed the agitation in Mosses and grew nervous. Mosses did much of the pressing in the shop and seemed never to look up from his work in customers were in the store.

"No, ma'am, we have not raised any prices in over two years.

All our customers would go to the larger cleaner if we did."

The old woman gathered her goods and gave a slight smile as if that was the answer she wanted to hear.

"You have got to contact the handler and pull the plug on this operation." Mosses pleaded as the three gathered in the small office in the rear of the cleaners.

"Has our cover been blown? What did you learn at the mosque today?" Jacob asked, dropping the fake middle eastern accent he used for his cover.

"No, my cover was not blown. In fact, I now know where the bank we are looking for is located.

The man I have been shadowing was there today, and I have his trust." Mosses swallowed and gasped like he was having trouble breathing. There was clearly more to be said, but the rush of information was overwhelming.

"Then this is good news." Marta defined.

"Not at all. The reason he trusts me is that they have been following us, and they believe we are genuine terrorists because the is a federal team watching us too.

"Protection?" Marta hypothesized.

"He says they look like an extraction team. He has seen plenty in the middle east. Most likely private contractors."

"Limited private contractors are operating on US soil." Jacob looked confused.

The chime of the little bell over the door alerting to

the entry of a customer sounded, and the three came forward.

"We give a discount to first responders," Marta called out as she led the trio out of the small office. Her offer came with her straining to speak understandable English. There were four people dressed in city police uniforms standing facing the counter. As a trained agent, she knew there was something wrong. Live through this encounter, Marta thought. Don't break the cover. Marta began to assess. They were not just standing randomly. They were covering the room. Some sort of tactical formation. The look on their faces was focused; they were ready for a rough encounter. And even though their uniforms and badges said ST. Louis City Police, they were carrying the wrong type of weapons.

"We did not come to get our clothes pressed. We had a few questions." The tall, strong-looking man in his forties spoke. He had a pockmarked face and a steely gaze like he was reading a map that was sitting too far away.

There were two other male officers and two female officers in the cleaners. An additional male officer could be seen through the storefront window guarding the entrance to the cleaners. A stocky pale-skinned female officer with a red buzz cut started to walk behind the counter, and Moses blocked her.

"Step aside, Sambo," Red commanded.

Mosses stood there staring straight ahead and not moving. He had endured many racial insults in the military academy and knew them for what they were.

"Relax, Mosses, we have nothing to hide," Jacob called to Mosses.

"That's right Nigger Jim, be a good nigger and step aside, and while you are at it, show me some ID. And it had better not be your grandmother's food stamp card."

"It is not necessary to insult him," Jacob shouted from the back of the room.

"I tell you what, why do you all pony up some current valid ID." The officer in charge commanded.

Red and Mosses still seemed locked in, staring at each other. Red made a half turn to fake, then spun around to punch Mosses in the face.

Mosses had boxed golden gloves before being accepted at West Point. Mosses slipped her punch and let the force from the would-be blow cause her to fall off balance and almost hit the floor. The other officers found this entertaining. Red did not. Red raced toward Mosses to grab him and wrestle him, but he held up the heel of his hand, and it hit her like the force of running full speed into a wall. She dropped to her knees.

"Stop this shit. The kid is clearly not trained to stand still and take a beating. No peaceful protesting or singing we shall overcome while you beat the shit out of him.' The commander praised the skill level of Mosses. Moses leaned forward to help the female officer up; the universal no harm intended move. She lay half kneeling and nursing a nosebleed. Then something Mosses had never before experienced overtook him. The light in the room seemed to dim, and a rush of air seemed to pass his ears. For a moment, he could swear he heard the voice of his late grandmother singing one of the old negro spirituals she used to sign on her way to church in Georgia. Mosses looked over at Marta and could not identify the look on her face, but she was staring at him. His midsection to be more precise. It hurt. He looked down at his midsection, and there was Red's hand. She had something in it. It was the handle of a knife, and the blade was buried deep within his stomach.

Mosses was sad not that he knew he was dying but that he had let Marta and Jacob down. He was the youngest of the team, and his inexperience was marring the operation. There was screaming from behind him. Then the screaming stopped at the end of automatic gunfire. It was Jacob that had been silenced.

"Bag the bodies if there is a bounty on either of them, I want us to get it. Bag the chick." The commander ordered. "And call the translator team that was recommended let's see what this one has to say."

Marta felt the nylon tie bind her from the back as a dark see through hood was placed over her head. She felt an over personal and over aggressive searching of her person and one last statement rang in her ears. It was from the commander. "Alright boys and girls let's get the fuck out of her before the real cops show up."

"SO. THIS IS THE PART where I fold the whipped egg whites into the batter." Alexis stated to Vincent Garrison. Vincent felt proud that his daughter Lisa and his next-door neighbor's daughter Alexis love to get cooking lessons from him. He also tutored them both in math even though Lisa, being eighteen and preparing for college, was at a higher level than Alexis.

"Now the trick is to wait until the oil is just the right temperature before adding the batter. Corn oil works best for pancakes and canola if you don't have it but never use a meat rendering.

The smoke point is too low. It will burn your product and taste burned."

"Oh my God what are you doing." Lowell Waterman entered the room from the kitchen. The Waterman's are Vincent Garrisons neighbors. The Garrison back door has a keypad lock and Vincent insisted that all the Waterman's know the combination. Lowell entered with his nine-year-old son Donny.

"Cornflakes," Donny screamed, and the small copper-colored puppy named Cornflakes rushed out to greet his favorite playmate.

"Mr. Garrison is teaching me to make Mississippi Pecan Pancakes."

"Not that. Where is your robe?" Lowell scolded.

"Well, I was cooking, and it was warm. Besides, Mr. Garrison doesn't see me that way." She turned to Vincent. "Do you." Alexis stood wearing a nightshirt that was probably the perfect size two years ago but now looked like she was blossoming in all the right places.

Vincent walked over to where Alexis had left the robe and handed it to her. "It is not about how I look at you. It is about your father asking you to do something and you questioning it. Do what he asks first. Then ask your question. The time we fathers have with our daughters goes so fast it need not be marred with defiance."

"God, I am sorry, Daddy. Sit, and you can be my first customer."

Lowell shot Vincent a look of gratitude for the parental backup.

"Oh my," Lowell exclaimed as he tasted the pancakes. "Why aren't you teaching my wife to cook."

"Because she is hopeless," Alexis mumbled.

"I heard that." Sharon Waterman explained, appearing from the kitchen in search of her missing family. "You are a traitor, Lowell Waterman. I send you to retrieve my children, and I find you eating pancakes."

"It was my duty as a parent to check her culinary progress.
And my God, are there good."

"Sit mom, you get the next batch."

"Mr. Garrison, Cornflakes says he wants to go outside to do his business," Donny called over the other conversation.

"Then, by all means take him outside, and maybe someday you can let me in on how the two of you talk to each other. It could save me countless carpet cleanings."

This brought a round of laughs from the group.

"Will Lisa be back soon?" Susan Waterman asked Vincent with a note of concern ringing in her voice.

"She is visiting her mom in Chicago. She should be back tomorrow. I keep thinking she will be off to college soon, and my nest will be empty." Vincent may have started the statement to be glib, but his eyes gave him away.

# Chapter 2

Vincent parked his car and walked to the waiting Toyota 4Runner. Barney sat behind the wheel. Rita sat in the back. The vehicle was parked in the rear parking lot of the First Baptish Church, their usual planned meeting place. Vincent took the front passenger's seat and handed the driving instructions to Barney.

"So that's it. Don't we talk." Impatiently Rita squeaked from the back seat.

"Look you guys know how I feel about you. I am grateful for everything you guys have done.

We have saved each other's asses too many times to count. But this is where I come out. No more missions. No more dirty and dark meetings.

"What about the Evil Queen. How is she taking your leaving to be a normal person?" Rita asked.

"Doesn't really matter. We broke off all romantic relations." Vincent answered in a dry voice.

"Romance, is that what you call it?" Barney remarked shifting the vehicle into drive and starting the journey.

"Who are we supporting? I hope it's the Navy. Those guys are cute, and they have manners." Rita queried.

"Private contractors dropped the ball, so we got the call. We are close, and I agreed to one last ride. But it was mostly because I wanted to see you guy ugly faces one last time."

They drove for a while, recanting tales of saving each other in close calls, and finally, Barney spoke out. "Did you check these directions?"

"Why, what's up?"

"If you have a perfectly good airbase, Scott Airforce Base, for example, why are we going to the back of East St. Louis?"

"I told you guys that's why I hate working with private contractors. Mercenaries.

They are probably holding shop in the back of a no-name strip club." Rita assessed.

"Remember our rule. We don't care if other teams are not professional, we are." Vincent attempted to calm the mounting restlessness of Rita as they drove the ragged streets of East St. Louis.

"How could there really be these many potholes. I moved to the right to miss one and hit a bigger one on the left. This is destroying this vehicle." Barney's level of agitation was starting to mount.

They dove down Missouri Avenue and turned and drove over a rusted bridge that looked like there was no way it could still safely be in use. The trip took them to Bond Avenue which, even though it seemed like a truly ragged street, seemed pristine compared to the street were they turned left. The was no sign indicating the name of the street. It was filled with huge potholes. Ragged burned out shack lined both sides of the streets.

"I aint giving up my gun I don't care who ask so if these guys ask for it, I will wait in the car." Rita proclaimed to no one in particular.

The dimness of the evening had begun to fall in front of them; there was a dilapidated structure that had once been a no-tell motel.

They could hear a dog barking, but the lack of people and solid structures made the barking echo and there was no telling where the barking was coming from.

"That, folks, is our destination." Barney pointed at the closed, broken-down motel.

As Barney eased up to the dilapidated structure, a short, muscular man carrying a machine gun stepped out. "ID, please." A woman with a red buzz cut appeared on the car's passenger side and signaled for Vincent to lower the window. Vincent lowered the window and handed her his ID at the same time Barney was showing his.

"Your friend is kind of cute for a Nigger." Buzz cut assessed Barney.

"We really have been trying to phase the word out.

It is overused and losing its primary effectiveness." Barney offered, and Buzz cut just looked confused. Rita handed Buzz cut her ID. Buzz cut, kissed the ID, and handed it back to Rita, then looked at Vincent. "I don't know why you let the hot little chili pepper ride in the back. I would have had her riding my lap."

'Room 9 straight ahead." The man with the machine gun instructed, tapping the vehicle on the roof.

"I am referred to as Cornel Norris. As you may have assessed, I am charged with collecting waste from various service branches and making it useful in operations. Sometimes this works well, and other times there are messes that need to be cleaned up." Cornel Norris was the commander from the raid at the cleaners. The room he had converted to be his office smelled of mold, rot, and urine. The furniture was to various degrees of broken. He had a big desk that had probably been moved from the main office of the motel and looked like an antique hunter's dream.

"Surrender, your weapons," Norris instructed.

Rita turned to Vincent and Barney. "Sorry boys this is where I get off. I am going to wait in the car. If the Cornel has a problem with that, I am walking home. I just hope I got enough bullets to make it back to civilization."

"You leave, we all leave," Vincent stated in a leadership tone.

"Keep your side arms with the understanding that if one of you draws one, you all pay the price." Cornel Norris made no attempt to vail his threat. "We were told there is a bank in the area. This is a place where terrorists on the run walk in one door and walk out the other with money and a new identity. We believe our quest knows the location of this bank."

"We were told you had three guests," Barney questioned.

"Two did not survive the trip." Norris led them around the desk and out to a room that was guarded by another of the cornel's men.

When he opened the door, light flowed slowly across the room, and something in the room scurried to cover the darkest corner. It took the team a moment to realize what they saw was human. Her eyes begged for help and the minimum of human kindness. She was naked and covered in blood and human waste. She looked frightened and lost.

"Alright, guys, this is the part where anything with a dick waits outside," Rita commanded, surveying the faces of the men with her. "Now!"

Rita dressed Marta's wounds and cleaned her up. Rita insisted that the clothes be located for Marta.

Rita and Vincent were interviewed without the presence of the Cornel or his guards.

"Al-Salam alikam." Vincent began when he was sure he was alone with Marta. She stared at him and gave no response. "Have you been violated? Are you hungry?" Vincent asked in Arabic. Still, there was no response, one her staring. "This smells like a total fuck up."

Vincent mumbled in English.

"You have no idea," Marta responded in Arabic.

Their eyes locked. There was a moment of recognition between the two. Wrong syntax and wrong stress on the words, and Vincent caught it immediately. She had learned textbook Arabic not what you learned growing up in the middle east.

"Lady, who the hell are you?"

"Right now, I am a woman who wants to stay alive. If I fail at that, I would like to keep you and your interpreter team alive." Marta responded in clear English with no accent.

"What did you find out?" The Cornel asked as Vincent, Barney, and Rita as the trio preprepared to leave.

"Remember the story when you were a kid about the goose that laid golden eggs." Vincent's question forced a confused look on his face. "One of your misfits may have killed the person who knew where the bank is before he could tell the other in his cell. It may take some questioning to

retrace where and when the person that located your bank found it."

IT HAD BEEN HARD FOR Vincent, Rita, and Barney to follow protocol, but they all knew the harder it was to follow protocol, the more important it was that protocol be followed. They had not spoken a word since giving the Cornel a false report.

Barney scanned the Toyota for tracking and listening devices, then checked their possessions and their persons. Now it was time to discuss tonight's disaster.

"I don't feel right leaving her back there with those animals." Rita broke the silence.

"I hate it too, but even she said it had to be done."

Vincent tried to reassure Rita. "Besides, my first obligation is to this team. If we had told them how bad they messed up, they may have needed to bury the evidence, which includes us."

"How could an operation go so off course? A mercenary strike team is attacking a fake government terrorist dummy site. And dead bodies." Barney paced for a moment, then completed the thought. "What if the misdirection was on purpose."

"Hold on, Barney, that would mean we are being played as pawns in a spy game. All our lives are in danger." Frantically Rita interjected, visualizing the beaten Marta humiliated in the darkness.

"So, I need you and Barney to start the report I will contact Ruth and bring her up to speed." Vincent did not like what he had just said but he knew it was for the best.

Ruth has their handler, and she has jurisdiction over the assignment. He and Ruth had been sleeping together off and on, and all the bad things that can come with sleeping with your boss had befallen him. This they had agreed, was his last job for her. His debt was paid in full. Lisa was now his daughter, free and clear.

"What say we sleep with our Glocks under our pillows until we get that report in the right hands," Barney suggested. Not only was Barney their technician, but he also had more experience in clandestine operations then they did.

# Chapter 3

It had not taken Barney long to compile his field report as he sat in his central west end apartment fighting back the sights, sounds and smells of the horror he had witnessed. Usually, the team worked with soldiers or civilians that were returning from a traumatic event and there was a dire need to collect data before the subjects we passed to the next stage of process.

Whatever that meant. Rita's email pinged Barney and he knew she had not chosen to sleep before she could finish her physical assessment of the recovered suspect. Barney attached the two reports then forwarded them to the Secured Federal Collection Servers that was assigned to the team.

Serena, Barneys live in girlfriend had already retired for the evening. Barney stood by the bed undressing and staring at his sleeping lover. One small lie he thought. One small lie about where he worked, and it had led to so many other lies. The clandestine nature of his work and the secrets. Oh, the secrets, not only his but also those of everyone he knew. Serena was a fitness instructor who specialized in getting women back into shape that had gained large amounts of weight over the years and was ready to turn their entire lives over to someone to make a change. There she lay, he thought. He had been begging her to marry him, and she had told him she was not ready for marriage, but if he wanted a child, she would be willing and proud to mother that child.

When did the world change so much, he thought, slipping into bed beside her? Barney had drifted off for what seemed only a moment when he heard a click. He reached for the nightstand where he kept his Glock 19, but as he opened his eyes, there were the eyes of the Redhead with the buzz cut he had met earlier that evening. On the side of the bed, there was also a man in tactical gear holding Serena. Serena's mouth had been duck taped, but the terror in her eyes spoke so loudly there was no need for words.

"That is one impressive piece of meat there, colored boy."

Red commented as she snatched the remaining covers from Barney. Barney lunged forward to grab her and felt a sharp stick from a syringe in his thigh.

Barney fought to stay consensus and did so just long enough to see the blurred haze of the man holding Serena slide a K-bar, a military combat knife under her rib to pierce her heart. The light in her eyes grew dim. He knew the darkness was his sanctuary.

"DID YOU HEAR THAT?" Sharon Waterman did not have to be a light sleeper to hear what could have only been a gunshot coming from the Garrison home. And before Lowell could answer, there were three more. The shots were not the small pop caused by small caliber weapons like .22 or .25 or even .32. Instead, the shots were the load clear beckon to death sound of a .45 or larger weapon.

"Call the cops. I am going over there." Lowell sprang from the bed and reached into the bedroom closet and retrieved a duck hunting shotgun that he had not used in many years. It was an old fire spitting overly loud and cheaply made hand-me-down.

"Maybe we should wait for the cops. That's their job."

Sharon said in a frightened voice.

"If someone is robbing the place, they probably took off after those loud shots. I can't stand to lie here thinking Vincent might be bleeding out on the floor."

# Chapter 4

"Now, you said you cooked breakfast with your next-door neighbor this morning before your family woke up. Are you frequently meeting your neighbor privately?" A strong-looking female officer with a name tag that read Baker asked Alexis. Two officers were questioning Alexis and her mother in the Waterman home.

The uniformed officers were the first to respond to Sharon's call. The Garrison home was now a crime scene.

"Mom, why is she trying to ask me stuff in that way?"

Alexis looked to her mother for support. Sharon stood shaking, thinking of the sight of Lowell being carried out on a stretcher and her not being allowed to leave the scene to go with him.

"What about you, ma'am? Has your single next-door neighbor perhaps prepared a few private meals for you?" Baker did not attempt to hide the lasciviousness in her accusation.

"Outside." A woman's voice screamed.

The command came from a slender woman who had entered the home. The woman had long, dirty blonde hair with a self-perm that was weeks past its life. She wore a tan raincoat covering a worn blue pantsuit.

The woman entering was Detective Dana Bullworth.

Detective Bullworth was followed closely by Miguel Micky Santiago, her partner.

Officer Baker turned to address Detective Bullworth. "We were first on the scene."

"Shut up. One more word out of you, and I will have you dragged out of here in cuffs.

Do you understand?"

Baker looked at her partner, a young, fresh-faced officer recently out of the academy.

"Son, I want you to walk your partner outside and find the Sargent on duty. Wait for us outside." Mickey instructed the young officer. There was clearly more Baker wanted to say, be she reluctantly followed her partner outside.

"What is this some kind of good cop bad cop like on tv?"

Sharon asked Detective Santiago.

Dana went and stood by the window and looked out.

This was the part of the operation that she was no good at, and she knew it.

"No games, no tricks. I hear your husband is in the hospital, and you want to see him. I will have someone drive you there and bring you back, but I do need to ask a few questions first." Micky smiled a little and then looked at Alexis. "I bet you are sixteen."

"How did you know." She said with all the amazement of someone seeing their first magic trick.

"Well, I have two daughters. One is sixteen, and I learn a lot from her. You kind of remind me of her."

"You learn from her?" Alexis had to have more.

Donny sat on the floor in a corner looking at Dana.

She wondered if he knew how uncomfortable it made her to try and be nice when she did not feel like being nice.

"His name is Cornflakes." Donny referred to the puppy who was shivering in the little boy's grip.

"He is afraid of loud noises and the shot gun hurt his ears." Donny sated moving closer to where his mother, his sister and now Micky was.

"Yes, see she tells me a know a lot but sometimes I say things wrong." Micky further explained to Alexis and motioned the small group to the couch and sat with them. "I need to ask some questions but if I use the wrong words or ask in the wrong way will you help me understand where I am getting off track?"

Alexis nodded, feeling a certain parental comfort with Micky. Dana stood silently by the window. This was a part of the job that Micky excelled in, and she did not. Micky turned a field interview with potential suspects into a meeting of a family friend. Micky had a way of learning twice what would have been learned using the heavy-handed method Baker had employed. In no time at all Micky and not only collect the information but he also had calmed down both Alexis and Sharon.

After seeing Alexis, Sharon, Donny and Cornflakes safety off with a couple of officers Dana and Micky walked through the field of police, technicians and news people that had collected. Baker and her partner stood by one police car with their Sargent.

Dana knew him as Sargent Randel.

Dana walked up to Randel and stood face to face with him.

"The book says that in this type of crime the neighbors are most likely involved." Baker sprouted.

"Sargent do you have one of your blue suits assigned to tell detectives what it says in the book?" Dana screamed into the Sargent's face in a way that stopped everyone around looking at them.

"NO Ma'am." The Sargent yelled back.

"Sargent does your average blue suit have any idea how hard it is for detectives to question let alone assess the mood and attitude of suspects after they have been subjected to what they feel is harassment by officers?"

"No Ma'am I would say not."

"Sargent are you capable of handling anyone under your command that is disrespectful to the detective in charge of a major criminal investigation?"

"Detective consider the matter handled." The Sargent motioned for Baker and her partner to get into their car. As Dana turned and started walking to the Garrison home the Sargent ran to Micky. "Hey, Santiago, why not through a guy a little rope from time to time."

"Sargent some night when you are in a dark alley, and some jacked up thug with a gun in cornered in an alley. And he recites those famous words. I would rather die than let you take me in. Tell me."

Micky stopped and smiled. "When you look to your right and see the cop standing next to you, would you rather my partner be there or a cop who can't survive a good ass chewing."

"Got it." And the Sargent was off the discipline his officers.

"Thank you, Micky." Dana commented and the two surveyed the layout of the house. The was a huge blood splatter where Lowell had been shot and fallen. The was a chalk outline where a man in a tactical outfit had been shot and died on the spot.

There was a huge bloodstain on the stairs leading to the upstairs bedrooms. There were also what looked like drag marks leading from the blood stains on the stairs. Micky could not help but look at all the happy photos that decorated the room. Father and daughter. Even the picture of Alexis and Lisa.

"No pictures of the ex-wife." Micky commented.

"Gee I hope you don't find that surprising." Dana said in a sarcastic tone.

"You break up with someone the pictures don't just go up in smoke. At least not without help."

"Alright partner reenactment time." Dana announced and walked to the stairs. She could hear the team still working on the second floor of the house. "Homeowner hears a noise and reaching into his nightstand and pull out his trusty weapon."

"Which just happen to be a model 1911 competition level .45." Micky answered, "Not the rusted out never cleaned .22 most homeowners have."

"Mr. Homeowner sees the big guy in built proof vest and tactical gear and fire a shot to the face." Dana added.

"In the dark at better than 15 feet. Bulls eye or lucky guy." It was Micky's turn.

Dana pointed at two holes made by the forty-five in the was in the opposite direction. "Someone was with bad guy number one. We say bad guy number two. So, homeowner shoots at number two bad guy."

"Someone returned fire. I say bad guy three. Now the Waterman's say they only heard the shots from what we suspect to be the .45. Then the blast of Mr. Waterman's duck hunting shot gun. The holes in the wall near the step are automatic gunfire."

"Automatic silenced machine gun. Not a standard issue for home invaders." Dana commented.

"Thank God."

Micky commented.

"Hey if you guys are the Dicks in charge can you come up here when you get a chance?"

A voice called from upstairs.

"On our way. "Dana confirmed.

"Do you see the same problem I do?" Mickey asked.

"I do. "

"The neighbor hears the shots, grabs his gun, then lets himself in through the back door. They had all the time in the world to run out the front. They were looking for something, and when they did not find it, they took Mr. Homeowner."

"REALLY NICE HOUSE, don't you think?" Dr. Chung with the medical examiner's office confirmed once he had Dana and Micky upstairs. "If you look over there, that room has its own bathroom. Judging by the products, they're most likely young girls. The bathroom was probably added to give her, her own privacy."

"So."

Dana coached.

"Well, is there a lady of the house? One other than our teen beauty queen?"

"Chung, I don't know where you are going, but no. The neighbors agree he is a loner in that respect. Mrs. Waterman said she has tried to play matchmaker, but he refuses."

Micky answered.

"Well, I have here in this bag a pair of men's pajama pants I pulled out of his dirty clothes bin." The doctor produced a pair of men's pajama bottoms in a plastic bag.

"Double so," Dana said.

"Well, they are covered with lipstick and foundation makeup. I would hazard to guess that got there....."

"I get the picture. Even someone who hasn't had any in as long as I have can remember how you got makeup on a man's pajama bottoms." Dana interrupted.

"I am going to have someone pull the traps from the sink and shower and get a hair sample for the girl. If there is something spooky going on, we need to know. If not, no accusations that could get us sued." Micky revealed.

"Just want to be sure we are all on the same page." The doctor clarified his position.

It still took a mini eternity for Dana and Micky to review what the crime scene told them. Just as the laws of eligibility predicted, dawn had begun to peak through and proclaim its rein when they were leaving the Garrison home. Most of the carnival that had been there when they had first arrived was gone. Only a few diehard new reports remained to wait for the last-minute insights they could scavenge from the unintended utterances of two overworked souls.

As the pair walked toward the unmarked police vehicle they had arrived in, Dana finally felt free to remove her raincoat. The coat had nothing to do with the rain. She used to coat as a barrier between her clothing and the body fluids found at crime scenes. She had few clothes and protected them. Dana had been on the devastating end of a bad divorce for many years past, and just as she started to emerge from the wolf at the door, her mother fell victim to illness.

Dana's mother's illness was not totally unexpected. Her mother had spent a lifetime of hard drinking and a rough lifestyle. What was unexpected was that Dana was expected to play the boulting daughter to the tune of repelling herself back into a chasm of even more outstanding debt. The truest irony of all is that Dana was good at her job. Dana had inherited poor interpersonal skills, but as an investigator, it did not seem to hold her back. The thing that caused her to excel was Micky. Manuel Ortez Santiago II was Mickey's actual name.

Micky and Dana had been partners for over five years. They were paired because no one wanted to work with either of them.

Dana due to her grumpy disposition.

And Micky because of his depression.

At the time when the two became a team Micky was deeply depressed at the loss through cancer of his wife. Micky was left with two girls and his older sister moved into his house to help him cope. Fate had pulled off another of its sick practical jokes in that as a pair of investigators they were very good.

"Excuse me Detectives does this abduction have anything to do with the abduction of a black man in the central west end?" As Dana and Micky got into the car this question was the only question she had heard. Why. It came to her. Abduction.

That had to be the first time this word was being used. She looked around and caught a glimpse of the young reporter that had asked the question.

He had a smug grim. Then I know something you don't grim. The grim she loved to slap off someone's face. But Micky was driving, and slapping would have to wait.

"I say we go back to the station and enter names in NCIC and start our general searches.

Then I'll take you to breakfast.

Followed by dropping you off at home, and we can both get naps and clean up and start on this mess this evening.

How does that sound?" Micky suggested.

"Micky, who was that guy? The last guy to follow us to the car."

Micky thought for a moment. "Lester is his name. Why? Are you thinking about asking him out?"

"Breakfast sounds great, Micky, somewhere with corned beef hash and hash brown potatoes. I am starving." Dana stared out the passenger side window, not caring that she had ignored his last question and knowing it meant little to him that she did.

THIS WASN'T HER THING, and she knew. Spy craft was a totally different set of skills. She was a med student who graduated as a doctor and wanted a way to pay off her student loans. Now here she was trapped in a cat and mouse or even cat versus cat in something she could not even understand. Rita Reyes had been a doctor since she had started fixing her friends broken dolls as a little girl. But no doll could compare to the sadness in the woman's eyes her team had been forced to leave behind.

"Oh, shit I win again." A large woman with a southern twang screamed out. Rita had found haven in one of the local casinos. It was based on something Barney had once told her about if you had to run. No extraction team worth their weight in sand would come anywhere near a Casio. They are open twenty-four hours a day with people constantly coming and going, they have an endless supply of surveillance cameras. Just the thing she needs to give her a moment to think. The loud noise and the constant bells, whistles and clangs of the Casio made Rita sure she would not dose off. The prior evening after she had emailed the copy of her report to Barney, she tried to call him. Rita knew it was a bad idea to call Barney so late. What if Serena got jealous. How would she explain the Barney had listened to her and helped her through a bad break up and she just wanted to hear his voice to chase away the evil she had seen.

But when there was no answer, she went to drive past Barneys house and there she saw it. A busted play. There were cops and stretchers and news people. Leaving the area of Barneys apartment Rita found herself in a maze of traffic outside Vincent's home. It was then she realized it. Barney had not been paranoid. There was an operation that was out of control and her team of basically support persons was trapped in the middle. Protocol dictated that she checks in with Ruth, their handler. But if all instincts were correct this deserved some additional thinking. Ruth had grown more and more unstable in her actions since Vincent had started resisting her sexual interest. Rita watched a group of Asian women shoved into a blackjack table who seem to be having the time of their lives. It was no doubt part of a bachelorette celebration, and the women was all drunk.

But it was fun seeking drunk and no one was rude or obnoxious. I am so sorry, Rita thought to herself. In a recent dispute with Vincent, she had call him the boss's whore. Vincent had only warned her about overly attaching herself to Barney so soon after her break up her ex-boyfriend.

# Chapter 5

"**D**etectives Bullworth and Santiago we have guests. Detectives James and Cross from St. Louis City. They say you are requesting information on a case they caught just last night." Lieutenant Marlow Dana and Mickeys boss lead two sharply dress city detectives to the desk were Micky and Dana were reading through reports. "Are the cases connected to anything you two are working on?"

"We don't know yet. We were eliminating a few things." Micky led.

"What was the victim's name?" Dana asked.

"Serena Poole. Real nice looking black girl. A fitness and nutrition coach. Specialized in slimming down fat women and making them useful to society" Cross answered.

It was difficult at this point for those who did not know him if insulting women in general was real or part of his technique to throw people off balance.

"How did it go down?" Micky asked.

"Well, we think the boyfriend came home and sniffed her panties and smelled the scent of another stud and stab her then disappeared into the mist." James offered.

"What was the boyfriends name?" Dana asked.

"Well, that's why we came in person." Cross started looking at Marlow for support. "The name he has been using is Barney Greer and he has ID that says that's who he is but."

"But Barney Greer, an airborne ranger with the 101 died five years ago in a training accident in Fort Bragg." James filled in.

"How could that be?" Marlow asked.

"When he finds the answer be sure to let us know because we ran the missing homeowner Vincent Garrison, and it would appear he arrived on this planet about 10 years ago as did his daughter." Dana held up the reports she and Micky had been reading and rereading when the group showed up at their desk.

"Fake ID?"

Marlow guessed.

"Birth certificates, driver's license, social security card, and passports all look as real as anything I have ever seen, but they are all bogus." Micky explained. "I have a suggestion. It looks like the trail leading to the county, so you copy us on anything you find or have. We copy you on what we find."

"Who gets the bust?" James asked.

"We split the credit if there is any. If we find the two crimes are unrelated you get a case half completed, in the meantime you get to spend time on your other cases." Dana offered.

"I like it."

Cross fired out.

"Look there is no blank check on hours around here you clowns show some progress or pass this to the feds. Body armor and machine guns sound like something right up their alley." Marlow finalized the arrangement.

# Chapter 6

"What exactly does Mr. Garrison do around here?" Micky asked Ruth Miller. Micky and Dana knew their first task was to separate the real Vincent Garrison from the fake one. They had traced his source of employment to Hollywell and Bradford holdings. The address listed was in a downtown office building that was a maze of small offices for various practices. Ruth Miller had received them and invited them to sit in her plush carpet office. There was something about the office that gave Dana and Micky a chill, and they did not need to confer to know it was mutual—the lack of homeliness. There were no diplomas on the walls or family pictures anywhere to be seen. Everything in the office looked like it came with the contract, and the renter was free to walk out and never come back.

"Vincent doesn't exactly work out of this office.

I mean he doesn't sell hamburgers out of a little window wearing a paper hat. Large companies buy up other companies, and often they inherit satellite companies. His job was to assess the value of those satellites. Make them profitable if possible or find a buyer if they have become redundant by the merger. He is quite the genus."

Ruth's response's gruffness sent Dana's natural grumpiness into overdrive. "Well, how long has he been working for you, or is that too hard a question?"

"About ten years."

"When the spaceship first landed?" Dana commented.

"What?"

"Never mind. Did you know him prior to his coming to work for you?" Micky tried to salvage the questioning.

"Were you seeing him socially?" Dana asked.

"What would that have to do with his disappearance?"

"Hopefully nothing but we plan to meet his daughter soon and we would appreciate any insights to her character." Micky offered.

"She doesn't like me. She is too clingy for a girl her age. She should be somewhere letting some young college guy feel her up in the back seat of a car. Instead, she is the perfect daughter never wanting him out of her sight."

"How long had the two of you been sleeping together?" Dana asked.

"Leave."

Ruth screamed.

"I am sorry, have I offended you? It's obvious that you are romantically interested in him. What happened did he shut you off? Maybe he found something a little spryer?" Dana asked.

Ruth looked at Micky with a cold hard-to-read look and slowly told him. "Walk this bitch out of my office if you value her in the least."

"Ma'am I certainly apologize for my partner she doesn't have the best social skills."

Mickey took Dana by the arm and began walking with her toward the door, the stopped and turned around. "Oh, I almost forgot since it probably has nothing to do with what we are working on.

Did Barney Greer and Vincent work closely often?"

"As I said Vincent is a genus, he picks his own team based on their skill set."

"I THINK IT IS SAD YOU get such joy apologizing for me, Detective Santiago."

Dana joked once the two were secured with the unmarked police car.

"And we now know there is a connection between Barneys missing and Vincent Garrisons missing. We need to call the city cops and tell them there is something going on and they need to reframe from giving any information to the news media just yet."

"What are you thinking?"

"There may be a reason outside our paygrade that these guys are missing."

"I hope that evil bitch is guilty of something we can arrest her on. I wonder if there is a law on the books about fucking the help."

"Let's hope not." Micky mumbled.

"Sorry Micky I forget, and I have a way of putting my foot in my mouth." Dana had forgotten that Micky had slept with Lt. Marlow a few times after his wife had passed when Marlow was going through a divorce.

Micky and Marlow had decided not to pursue the relationship because of its complications but still had great respect for each other.

# Chapter 7

"Hello, Alexis." Micky greeted Alexis outside the non-denominational chapel at Barnes Jewish Hospital. Alexis was seated, staring at the floor. When Dana and Micky sat beside her, she seemed almost not to notice.

"Alexis, remember when I told you I have a daughter much like what I see in you."

Alexis smiled, fighting back tears.

"Well, my daughter Maria is a good girl. But she is known to keep confidence."

"Do you think that is bad?" Alexis whispered.

"No. It means that your first choice is not to gossip about other people's business, and that is the sign of a true friend."

"I think I understand. You know, there is something I know about Lisa and her father, and I don't feel right talking about it. You see, Lisa is like a big sister to me, and she has helped me to avoid a bunch of stupid choices."

Dana stood up and wandered into the chapel, where she was sure she would find Mrs. Waterman praying for her husband's recovery. It was an excellent point to leave Micky to what he did best.

"If there weren't a chance that Mr. Garrisons' life was on the line, I would never dream of asking you to break a confidence. But your friend Lisa will be home soon, and she will want to feel that everything possible is being done to find her father. I can't say she won't be mad at you for telling me. Especially at first, but I understand you might lose your father. Do you want her to feel she has lost hers too and there everything possible wasn't done to save him."

"The secret is he is not her natural father. He adopted her as a child."

"She goes to visit her mother in Chicago."

"Not really.

Lisa saw her real mother and father die in front of her. The big part of the secret is that Lisa goes to Chicago to see a doctor."

"Is she ill?"

"The doctor is a psychiatrist. I only know the doctor is a woman who deals in something called LTE. I told her it sounded like a venereal disease, and she said Well at least if she caught one or those, she would have had fun getting it. Right up to the point where her father found out." Alexis seemed a little more relieved, having unburdened herself to Micky.

"I trust the two of you were having a good visit." Mrs. Waterman said to Micky with a slight note of suspicion in her voice as she exited the chapel with Dana and Donny.

"Mom, Micky was telling about his daughter Maria while we waited for you."

"Please refer to him as Detective Santiago. He has probably done a great deal to earn that title."

"Yes, Mom."

"They say my husband will probably live and will never be quite the same as he was.

Few people that are machine-gunned are." There was residual anger in Mrs. Waterman's voice. "My husband did what his principles told him to do. Now find the bastards that did this to him and make them pay." With Mrs. Waterman's last comment, she stared into the eyes of Dana, where she knew the resolve to do harm to others found its greatest resting place. No words were needed to be exchanged between the women. The deal had been secured.

# Chapter 8

Two strong men in tactical gear dragged Vincent into the makeshift office of the man calling himself Cornel Norris. The blue of his eyes floated in the reddened backdrop of his iris. There was a half-finished bottle of a no-name bourbon on his desk, and his appearance showed clearly, he was a name lost to time of day or time zone, so he did what he wanted when the mood struck him. The strong men dropped the handcuffed and fastened Vincent into a steel frame chair facing the desk of the Cornel. Vincent was bruised and his clothes had been ripped to tatters.

In an incredibly short time, he was almost unrecognizable from Vincent that had taught breakfast cooking to his neighbor's daughter only hours ago.

"I was in Africa a few years ago. The guest of one of the tribal militias." The Cornel began as if he had been asked a question though none had been posed. "How are you feeling, Mr. Garrison?"

Vincent tried to form words, but his lip was too swollen from being hit in the face with a gun butt.

"I was starting to think I must be the most incompetent military mind on the planet when I got back results of the so-called terrorist using the name Mosses."

Vincent peered up through his swollen black eye. More information, he thought. This is the time I must hold back the pain and learn.

"His real name is Robert David Casswell III. He is a recent graduate of West Point on loan to one of the United States clandestine services." The Cornel poured whiskey into a dirty glass that sat in front of him. "Someone fucked me."

Vincent wanted to laugh, but he and to choose between breathing or laughing, and breathing won out.

"Whores get paid. I'll take the bank. I want you to go in there and get that woman's confidence, whoever the fuck she is, and have her tell you everywhere Moses or whoever he was went. I want you to find out where he was returning from and where that bank is."

Vincent looked up, reading the man. Knowing it was all about life and death now.

"I mentioned Africa. Well, there was a man there whom the people sponsoring me wanted information, and he was quite resistant. So, the General of the militia tied the man's wife faced down to a table and stripped her waist down. He had his men line up and take turns."

Horror overtook Vincent's face as a translator; he had heard stories far worse.

"The woman was bound in such a way that the man could watch the pain in his wife's face.

I did not understand why the General asked no questions. Then it all became crystal clear when the General untied the wife and strapped down the man's ten-year-old daughter. There was no need to even touch the little girl beyond tying her up. The way the man's wife looked at him told him he had to spill his guts. Any questions asked, he answered."

In the distance, maybe 100 yards away, Vincent could hear the lonesome hobo call of a train.

Civilization, as Rita had described it, was at least 100 yards too far. He would have to make the best decisions he could, knowing none would be perfect.

"I understand you have a daughter." The Cornel said in a matter-of-fact way just before gulping down the dirty whiskey.

# Chapter 9

"Did you see that?" Dana asked Micky as they drove up to the Garrison home. The Garrison home has a detached garage in the back and there was movement that Dana spotted.

"I am calling back up just in case our friends with the machine guns are searching the place," Micky announced. Before he could get his location completed into the handheld walkie-talkie, Dana had left the vehicle and was heading for the side door of the garage. The slightly off-track door made a slight squealing, and Dana slowly opened the door with her gun in her right hand. As she slowly entered the darkened garage, she panned the room full of junk, pointing the barrel of her .9mm.

"Easy.

Take your finger off the trigger and step back slowly." Someone had pointed a gun at the back of Dana's head and put one hand on her shoulder.

The voice was a hushed whisper, but it was that of a young lady.

"I'm a cop."

Dana mildly protested.

"Good, then it will save me the time of explaining what will happen to the top of your head when I pull the trigger on this Glock." To emphasize her point, the girl poked Dana with the gun barrel.

"Now the guy with you is trying to angle me; tell him to enter the room slowly."

Dana did not like this at all. The girl seemed to know more than the average person about how cops operate. Before Dana could decide, Micky slowly walked into the door with his gun pointed toward the girl holding the gun to Dana's head.

"Are you the creeps that have my dad?"

"No. We are cops trying to find him."

"How do I know that?"

"Why don't I show you, my badge." Dana reached toward her inner jacket pocket with her left hand, and the girl grabbed tightly with one hand and smacked the gun barrel into the back of Dana's head.

"Look, don't fucking move. Let me tell you what is going to happen the next time you so much as twitch. I am going to put one in your brainpan, then drop to a crouching shooting position and empty the remaining rounds toward your boyfriend. Now I am fairly sure I will kill him even if it means he kills me. But what the fuck would you care because you will be long dead."

"Fuck this little bitch Micky. Shoot." Dana angrily instructed.

"That's right, Micky. Shoot." The girl repeated the command.

"Are you Lisa?" Micky asked.

"So, you know my name."

"Alexis told me you are the closest thing she has to a big sister. She said you talked her out of a bunch of stupid decisions."

Lisa took her left hand off Dana's shoulder and retried a cell phone. She pressed a preloaded number. Micky was sure what she was doing, but backup would arrive soon, and the situation's dynamics would change. He was frightened for Dana, who seemed not concerned for herself.

"Operator 1404 code 147," Lisa called into the phone.

Someone on the phone spoke briefly with Lisa as she continued to watch Dana and Micky.

"Here."

Lisa handed the phone to Dana over her left shoulder.

The person on the line had Dana give her badge number and ask a few questions.

There was the flashing of lights from outside of the detached garage. The uniformed police had arrived. Soon they would make their way back to the garage.

Dana handed the phone back to Lisa, as the person on the phone had instructed. Lisa listened for a moment to the person on the phone, then disconnected. She then laid her gun down on a stack of boxes that was cluttering the garage. Dana turned around in a flash and backhanded Lisa.

Lisa punched Dana hard in the face.

Dana smacked Lisa in the face with the gun butt; it did not have the desired effect; instead of subduing, Lisa seemed to go into a rage, bounding forward and locking her teeth on Dana's breasts.

Micky scrambled to separate them, but the grip of Lisa's teeth seemed to put Dana in great agony.

"God, Micky, get this crazy bitch off me." Dana cried out.

Two uniformed police heard the ruckus in the garage and ran to the Detective's rescue.

It took Micky and the two uniformed officers to get Lisa wholly restrained.

"What are you doing?" Micky asked Dana. After the uniformed officer had left with Lisa, Dana grabbed Micky and led him to one of the bathrooms in the Garrison home and closed the door. Dana began removing her blouse.

"I need you to take a look at this."

"Dana, I don't think I am the right person." Micky tried, but Dana blocked him from exiting the bathroom.

"Micky, you were married, and you have two daughters. I am sure at some point in your life; you saw a pair of tits."

The bite was pronounced and ragged. The area had started to swell and turn color. Micky started without thinking to palpate Dana's skin, then looked up at Dana, staring at him.

"I don't mind if you touch me, Micky."

"I'm taking you to a doctor; that's what you need."

"Yes, Micky. I try never to argue with a man while he has my breast in his hands."

"Just when this was starting to feel a little less weird."

They both got a mild chuckle out of his embarrassment.

"VINCENT, ARE WE DEAD?

Are we in hell?" Barney had started to come around. Marta had been trying to treat some of his wounds the best she could with one hand chained to a radiator.

Thery were in a filthy room in the condemned motel that was filled with garbage that even the crackhead prostitutes that once operated out of this motel could find no use for. Rats peeked out at them, then disappeared, biding their time.

The cornels men had dropped Vincent on the floor face down. "We are somewhere outside East St. Louis before Washington Park.

"I get it, so yes, we are in hell, but are we dead?"

Barney asked.

"Not yet."

"Good cause I am making a list of motherfuckers I will kill before I die. They killed Serena. It was like a joke to them. Just another day on the job."

"Your friend needs a doctor."

Marta stated, examining Barney. "What happened to the doctor that was with the two or you?"

"If she isn't here, they do not have her, and their sad luck is she is operational by now," Barney stated, spitting blood from the cuts in his mouth.

"If they went to grab her, they might not have been able to find a good time." Vincent looked at Marta. "Her brother is a St. Louis City cop, and they have been trying to set up rules for a charity poker tournament against the fire department."

"So."

"So, she had been staying at her brother's house since her break up. And with cops and firemen coming and going, it is a good bet she got on to the merch before they could snatch her."

"So, we wait?" Marta asked.

"They want me to manipulate you into telling me where Moses found the bank," Vincent explained to Marta.

"If all else fails, grab the money and run," Barney muttered, half-conscious.

"They plan to go after Lisa."

There was silence for a moment; it seemed the footfalls of the rats could be counted.

"Is she your wife?"

Marta finally asked.

"She's, my baby. She's, my world."

# Chapter 10

Rita's hand trembled as she wrestled the padlock on her storage locker. The locker had been rented by her brother in his name, he had insisted on it because he could use his military discount and save her money. Rita had Roberto rent the storage when she moved out on Jason, her former boyfriend. There in the storage locker in an unruly pile was the soul content of her life.

In the Casio hiding and trying to think of what had to be done next, she had formulated part of a plan. Right now, her greatest regret was that she wished she did not have a habit of talking over people so much. She had spoken over Barney often when he was trying to explain urban terrorist survival techniques to her.

There she found it.

Her old flip phone in a box with a charging cord. When the phone was charged, she would go to a busy spot where the cell towers most likely intersected and make her call. In the meantime, she would collect what she needed to survive. She had left her car parked at the Casio and had taken a bus to the storage locker. She pulled out her old ten-speed bicycle. I hope I am still in shape for this.

"MICKY, DO YOU MIND if I have a moment alone with your partner?" Lt. Marlow asked in a too-friendly tone.

"Not at all, boss. I was on my way to the lab anyway. Is there anything I should know?" Micky surveyed the faces of both women for a read that never came.

Micky and Dana had spent much of the morning preparing to question Lisa. They knew a lawyer was counseling Lisa and were not sure how far the questions would get or even if they would be helpful. It was essential to know who the man among the missing was.

"Just a little girl talk, nothing that concerns you." Marlow offer in an equally chilling attempt to sound matter of fact.

After the door to Marlow's office was closed, she walked over to Dana and whispered in her ear. "How is your arm?"

Dana fidgeted from the pain and discomfort. "Much better, thanks for asking, Boss."

"I have a report on my desk that says she bites you on the arm. She says she bites you on the tit. Can you explain the discrepancy?"

Dana stood shrouded in embarrassment she that was coming.

"Judging from your silence, I take it you want to think on that for a moment.

Good, let's move to the next question."

Marlow leaned even closer and whispered even softer. "Did you pistol whip a suspect that you knew had mental issues after she was surrendering?"

"Well, it was all sort of complicated at the moment."

"Listen to me, Detective Bullworth. Her lawyers are here; they have been chatting with her for the better part of the morning."

"But." Dana started to interrupt.

"Hell no, you do not get the privilege of interrupting after your fuck up. Do you know how many women there are in professional positions who struggle every day to be taken seriously? Under no circumstances am I losing my job over your cranky ass.

Do you realize the position you have put me in?" Marlow stopped and stared at Dana. "Even though the ship of romance may have sailed for me and Micky, I still love and respect him. There is no way I will let you drag him into the undertow." Marlow stopped talking and started pacing. It was like a fuse leading to the subsequent detonation. "Okay, here is how it works. I go into the interview with you, and we speak to the girl and her counsel. If they throw us a bone, we take it. If you insist on playing hard ass, my best bet may be to have you held for psychiatric observation.

"I AM MR. GORMAN, I will be representing Lisa Garrison from a criminal prosecution, and this is Ms. Shelton her firm will be handling civil matters regarding the beating of our client." A tall thin man with a well-manicured beard introduced a short, stocky woman with a decidedly judgmental stare. When the guards led Lisa Garrison into the room, she looked nothing like the wild woman that wrestled with Dana. Whoever handled the wardrobe and fitting at the lock-up must have had the day off because Lisa's orange jumpsuit was easily two sizes too large and enveloped her in such a way that it made her look twelve years old. Her head had been bandaged with what looked like fifty feet of wrap.

Lisa looked so pathic Lieutenant Marlow could not help but stare at Dana. As soon as the small group was seated, Lisa said something in a delicate whisper that no one seemed to catch.

"What is it, baby?" Ms. Shelton asked.

"Where is Micky?" Lisa repeated a little louder.

"He has other work. This is a busy police station, and not everyone can stop their day to visit you." Dana said in a tone that aggravated Marlow.

"I would feel better if he was here. Can we get him or reschedule." Lisa asked.

"Why." Dana one-worded it.

"Well, I don't want to put words in a client's mouth but putting her in a room with the maniac that pistol-whipped her and not allowing the man who pulled the bitch off into the room would be my best choice of guesses." Ms. Shelton had a talent for getting under the skin of the police.

"Detective Bullworth, go find your partner, and I don't give a rat's ass what he is doing; get him in this room," Were the words Marlow used to silence the next thing Dana would say.

"HELLO, LISA," MICKY said as Dana led Micky into the room. The group had waited uncomfortably.

Finally, Lisa spoke. "Micky. I mean Detective Santiago."

"How are you, Lisa?"

"Well, I am alive, thanks to you."

"Oh, for fuck's sake, are you guys buying this shit?" Dana interjected.

"Detective, if you continue creating a hostile environment, I am going to have to ask you to leave the room," Marlow announced.

"It was all a misunderstanding. I overreacted, and so did your partner. Can we just skip the lawsuit stuff, and you guys go find my father."

"You need to rethink this, honey; if you drop charges against the police, they may choose to arrest you for resisting arrest and failure to head a lawful command."

Shelton spoke sourly to Lisa.

Lisa's head dropped forward, and she began to cry. "Damn these games, he is out there, and he needs me."

"Lisa, are you saying that if we promise not to press charges, you will drop your charges and answer a few questions that could get us close to finding him," Micky asked.

"Oh, God, yes, Micky. That's why I wanted you here. You are a family man; you know the hurt."

They all seemed to stop as if shifting gears. "I have a question." Dana began. "I only hope it doesn't get me sent to my room with no supper. But he really isn't your father, is he?"

"Lady, if I apologize for biting you, would you try not to word your questions in such a hurtful way? Yes, I am adopted. But he fed me since I was a baby. He dressed me and helped me with my homework. He sang to me when I was sick." A rush of tears now flooded Lisa. "How dare you say he is not my father."

"I have to ask this, but is there a physical relationship between you and Vincent Garrison?" Dana asked.

"I am sorry too, Lisa, but it is a question we would be negligent if we did not ask." Marlow, this time back Dana up.

"If you were guys, I would say don't be so quick to think with your dicks."

This made Mr. Gorman, who had remained silent, chuckle. "You see it don't you, Mr. Gorman? They are thinking with their vaginas."

Marlow looked at Micky, hoping he could shift the meeting back on course.

"You see it don't you, Micky."

"I do, but why don't you explain it to them."

"Well, Micky has a nine-year-old daughter named Isabella. What if something happened to Micky, and he perished?

What if the only person that could keep his daughter from slipping into a depression for which there was no return was you." Lisa stopped and stared at Dana. "Would you push her away? Would you tell doctors to drug her? She won't know the difference."

"How did you know the detective had a nine-year-old daughter named Isabella?" Marlow asked.

"Is there a prior relationship with the two of you the rest of us needs to be brought up to speed on?" Shelton asked.

"No." Micky and Lisa said simultaneously.

"I think I must have heard one the guard talking." Lisa smiled.

"The long and short of it is you can't hold her if you are not charging her."

Gorman proclaimed.

"I agree, but we have a dead body and a missing taxpayer. So, we will still need to ask questions." Marlow closed.

# Chapter 11

"You are requested to return to the nest." The automated voice told Rita on her flip phone. Rita had cycled to downtown St. Louis. There was ample hustle and bustle to hide anything. But the command needed to be corrected. One thing she could remember from Barney was that there is no way you can walk through the front door of your handler after a broken or busted play.

First, if someone was after you, that is the first place they would stake out. Second, if they were following you had an idea where to pick up your trail, you would be leading them to your base before they had a chance to clean house.

Damn, she thought. This is worse than I thought.

Rita walked into the small restaurant where her brother Roberto was having lunch. Roberto sat by himself with a large hamburger and a mountain of French fries in front of him.

Rita slid into the opposite side of the booth and sat down. She dumped ketchup on his fries and began shoveling them into her mouth. Roberto barely looked at her. The was a waitress that was eye-flirting with him from across the room, and he seemed more engrossed in the ritualistic practice.

"Roberto, I am in trouble, and I think I might need your help," Rita said, then picked up his hamburger and took a big bite.

"If you in trouble, that white boy better man up and marry you, or I am going to go loco on his ass. You left the house like a cat in heat and now."

Rita dropped the burger back on the plate and stared at him. The waitress came to the table. "Gee Roberto, your girlfriend is going to let you starve."

The waitress noted in a heavier accent than Roberto or Rita.

"She aint my girlfriend; she is my little sister, and she is a doctor."

"I'm going to get you another plate of food cause it don't look like they are feeding doctors these days."

The waitress walked away, and Roberto noticed Rita was still staring at him with a frozen look on her face. "It's a good thing Mama is dead, Roberto.

She doesn't have to hear you calling your baby sister a puta pintado. I mean, I would slap your face if you were not wearing that blue police uniform. Mama and Papa raised the men in this family to be good Catholic men. Good Catholic men respect the woman in their families.

This is why they sent me to medical school and not you." She started to stand up to leave.

"No, I am sorry. Stay and eat.

Explain the problem."

Rita quickly sat back down. "Well, there is this thing called a busted play."

"Like in football?"

"I don't know football, so maybe if I explain from the beginning. I am a doctor, right?"

"Yes, at the VA hospital."

"Yes, but I have been working as what is called a ground. In the spy world, there are agents that have fictitious backgrounds so sometimes, when they put together a team, they use a ground. The guy with fake pasts are live wires that need to be grounded to someone that can be checked from front to back and check out."

"I feel so much better you are telling me you are a spy. There I thought you were pregnant, and this sounds so much crazier." He put his head in his hands and shook it.

"Roberto, I am still your baby sister. I still am a doctor, I just needed to work on some patients, most of whom were soldiers with problems, and I had to go where they were with a team."

When Roberto moved his hand there, his look of dismay had been replaced with a look of pride. "What do you need?"

"Some people will come to you. Do not be too concerned about anything they say. They are masters of lying. They mix the truth with lies, and even a street cop may not be able to judge the good guys from the bad."

The waitress had returned with a plate of food to replace what Rita had eaten. "My brother wants to ask you out be he is too shy."

"I will go out with him if he asks. I got to have my pride too."

"Will you go out with me?" Roberto asked.

"Hell, yes, Roberto, you cute." And the waitress was gone.

# Chapter 19

Two men in tactical outfits dropped a large clothes bag in the middle of the floor in the room, being used as a jail cell for Vincent, Marta, and Barney. One of the men kicked the bag, and it jumped and screamed in pain, the scream of a woman. Barney crawled forward to help the next guest out of the bag.

"Agggggh, is that a rat?" Dr. Walker jumped into Barney's arms, not noticing he was almost bare after being taken at night.

"Rats. See, I told you, Vincent, those weren't the copper doodles we ordered."

Marta and Vincent joined Barney in a laugh.

"How can you laugh? We are prisoners. I was on my way to my car, and I heard a girl say hey, ma'am did you drop your wallet the next thing I knew, two giants were grabbing me, and the girl raised my skit and jabbed a needle in my thigh."

"Welcome to our private nightmare." Barney offered.

"I do remember one other thing. DeJohn, one of the parking lot attendants, tried to help me. And I remember bullets going through his body as he flew through the air."

"You need to get her ready, Vincent," Barney said in a severe tone.

"Ready? Ready for what I and a shrink, not a field agent." Miller protested.

"Doesn't matter; it's not our game, so we don't say who plays," Marta stated. Marta and gone into a corner and squatted on a pot they had given to use. Even the illusion of privacy had dissipated over the time the hostages spent together.

"Who is she? I don't know her. Is she an agent?" Suspiciously, Dr. Miller asked.

"We don't know who she is, and we don't want her to tell us. That is, one more lie we won't have to try to keep from Cornel Norris." Vincent offered. "Besides, whoever she is, there is no way for her to know we are who we say we are. If she is FBI, CIA, or NSA, she is trained not to trust."

"This could all be some form of an elaborate scheme to steal knowledge from her, and this blood on his may just be fake blood." Barney offered.

"What does he mean to get me ready?" Finally, Dr. Walker had to ask again.

"We figure that The Cornel has some information, but since his mission broke down, he is unsure where the disconnect or false intel is. So, he asks us questions individually, hoping to match what we tell him against what he knows is the truth." Vincent explained.

"So soon, he is going to drag you out of here and question you," Barney explained.

"That's ridiculous. I don't know shit about operations; I am a doctor. If you had not chosen to stop seeking my help, your daughter's doctor and your doctor."

"And I hope we have time to fight about that later, but now let me finish. Answer any question he may ask as truthfully as you can remember; he is not just questing you; he is matching answers."

"Will he kill me?"

"Not right away, he thinks we are lovers, and he wants to strap you to a table and make me watch his men rape you. But he wants my daughter to be there, so if I don't give in and tell him what he wants, they will rape her."

"That's crazy."

"Well, being the house expert on crazy, I will take your word for that."

"Why don't you tell him what he wants? People do it in the spy game all the time."

"Because my knowing what he wants to know is just as flawed as his thinking we are lovers."

For Dr. Walker, it was like the filthy room was spinning. There was an abstract logic to what was said. The logic they had kept the trio alive for so long. By telling only the truth, he could not locate where the flaw in the operation had occurred.

Then the door opened, and it was her time to face the Cornel.

DANA AND MICKY WALKED into the Cracker Barrel Restaurant and noticed how busy it was. Servers were rushing about at full speed. There were tables of customers in every type of uniform you could think of. There were a couple of tables of firefighters and a couple of tables of Missouri State Troopers.

Dana spotted the table they were looking for and led Micky to the table. "You must be Officer Roberto Reyes." Mickey acknowledged.

Roberto and Jerome were seated with two female uniformed officers.

"Check this shit out, dog. That fake FBI shit didn't work this morning, so they went and dusted off some old ass, Uncle Tom Mexican to gain my confidence." Roberto said to Jerome, ignoring Dana and Micky.

"Hey, Roberto, they are the real deal. I know cause that is the bitch that had me written up."

The officer that was on the first to respond at the Garrison's home called from a different table.

"I let you off light," Dana yelled back.

"How you figure?"

"I let you keep your teeth. You would be surprised how many are not that fortunate."

"SO, TELL ME THE TRUTH is my little sister some sort of secret agent?" Roberto asked after the three were outside.

"We don't think so. We think your sister did some support work for some guys doing high-level clearance stuff, and they are missing." Micky answered.

"Wow. So why don't she pick up the phone and call in more spies like we do for backup?" It was poorly stated, but it set both Dana and Micky thinking.

Micky reached into his pocket and handed Roberto his card. "I think she is having trouble knowing who she can trust on her own team and is trying to get in touch with us."

"Wow. Hey, sorry about the Uncle Tom Mexican thing."

Micky said nothing but gave Dana a wry smile.

# Chapter 20

"I almost forgot you were in there," Dana said to Jewel the doll as she discovered it looking for her phone in her purse. Dana and Micky had returned to his house. Micky had no words for anyone; he just went to his room and closed the door. "You have been trying to tell me something all day, right?" Jewel, the homemade doll, stared back with her mismatched button eyes.

"That is a sign that you are spending too much time with Isabella, talking to her doll." Dana turned around, and Maria was standing there in a night-shirt.

Maria had been in bed but wanted to wait until she could speak to Dana, and Dana knew it.

"I guess you want to talk," Dana said as they sat closely on the makeshift bed.

"Tell me about your mother, Ms. Dana." Maria requested.

"Well, do you know the difference between a whore and a prostitute?"

Maria looked shocked at the question and froze."

"Well, prostitutes sell it, and whores give it away.

My mother managed to combine both talents. Whatever or whenever she could not sell it, she gave it away."

"God, I feel so stupid having asked." Maria hugged Dana.

"I don't know who my father was, and I don't think my mother does either. That's what bothers me about this case your father and I are working on. The missing guy seems like a good dad. Your father is a great dad. But that is not enough to stop bad things from happening in their lives."

"Then he comes home and finds me letting some creep finger me in the driveway."

"Maria, just remember you never have to like or agree with anything your father says or does. You must remember he is doing it or saying it because he loves you. Once upon a time, I would have given my right arm to have a father there to scold me for doing something stupid." Dana offered.

"And you love him, don't you?"

"It's complicated."

"I don't understand, he loves you, and you love him."

Before Dana could formulate her next thought, let alone reply, her cell phone rang. She reached into the purse and retrieved it. "Yeah."

"I just left the doctor; my hand is broken, and you crushed some bones. I type for a living bitch." It was Lester.

"Sweetheart, we will have to finish our girl talk later. But know that I love you girls, and you are in my heart." Dana said and watched Maria leave the room.

"Well, I will tell you what, if I had known, exactly what you did, I would have cut your fingers off and made a necklace, your sick bastard."

Dana told Lester on the phone.

"Have you listened to the other tapes?"

"No, that's not how I get off."

"Look, I will make you a deal. Return the tapes to me without listening to them, and I won't press charge against you."

"Fuck you.'

"Return what is mine, and I won't press charges against your partner. I press charges against him, and some slick lawyer will do his best to make his daughter look like a slut in front of the world."

Where and when sleaze ball?"

"Millennium Park 9:00 am on the jungle gym, and don't bring your partner or I bolt. No way I let the two of you kick my ass again."

Dana crept down the hallway and lightly tapped Micky's closed bedroom door.

"Come in."

"If it's time for me to rub that funny-smelling stuff on you, I think you left it somewhere," Micky stated as Dana entered the room and sat beside him on the bed.

Dana told Micky about the call.

"Well, there is only one thing to do." Micky began.

"Yeah, listen to the tapes. And if necessary, make copies." Dana answered, slid into bed beside him, and began listening to the tapes.

DR. WALKER, NOW BOUND to a chair in the office of the man calling himself Cornel Norris, muttered the repeated phrase. "I am not a field agent; I only help them to recover." Her grey-laced blond hair, now matted with blood and mud, covered her face. The Cornel had asked the same questions, only varying how they were asked by little more than a word or two.

"If what you are telling me, someone had fed me faulty information from the very start and trapped me in this hell hole. And for your sake, you had better pray that I think you are lying because otherwise, that means you are one hundred and twenty pounds of dead weight and no use to me." He slapped her several times to get his point across, then signaled for her to be returned to the makeshift cell with his other prisoners. As Dr. Walker was dragged out and thrown back onto the cell floor, she wondered how the many field agents made it through such harsh treatment. In the distance, she could hear a train. There was life out there somewhere. She wondered if she would live to see it again. Poor DeJohn, she thought maybe the train she heard was in her mind carrying his soul to wherever its final destination would be.

DANA STROLLED ACROSS the grass leading to the jungle gym in Millennium Park.

She saw Lester waiting there in jeans and a hoodie. Dana felt more rested than she had in days she had not returned to Micky's sofa but had spent the night sleeping in bed with him. They had not had sex, but she held him as he slept, which felt good.

She also felt better about having invaded his life. In the morning, his sister, Rosa, had caught her trying to sneak out of Micky's bedroom before his girls could wake. Rosa gave Dana a wink.

Just as Dana was reaching Lester, he smiled his last greasy smile. A bullet tore through him and propelled him backward.

Dana looked around, and a man was standing what must have been one hundred yards away with a rifle. The man aimed the rifle at Dana, and she knew what she had to do. Dana had not yet been returned her service weapon since the shooting in her backyard.

Technically she had no business to be still working the case but did not feel she could rest somewhere while Micky was facing danger. Dana kicked off her shoes, reached into her purse, took out her backup weapon, and ran toward the shooter as fast as possible. Dana now knew the pistol she carried for a backup was useless as a pea shooter in a windstorm at this range. There was no time to check Lester. Everything she knew about gunshots told her he was no longer an issue. The man in the distance knew what Dana was doing; she was trying to get close enough to get a shot off at him. She would be dead, but so would he. It was a fearless last act of desperation, and she jumped to it without hesitation, sprinting the fastest she had ever run. The shooter smiled and winked, then pointed the rifle directly at Dana. Shoot the charging animal one perfect shot or die. Just as Dana raised the .9mm to fire, she heard a loud noise. It was the same loud sound she had heard the night of the shoot-out in her backyard.

But it had been so long since she had heard the sound she could not recognize in the backyard. There was also too much adrenaline pumping that night. But now, hearing it again after a rested night, she knew exactly what the sound was. It was right before the man fell out of the tree stand in her backyard.

The sound was the sound of a Barrette Arms .50 Caliber and the loud ejection when fired. In front of her, the man with the rifle's head exploded, and a pink mist blasted into the air. Dana stopped running so fast her brain did not get the signal to her legs quickly enough, and she slid down on the ground in the grass. Dana looked off to her right, and Drake was putting the heavy-looking .50 caliber in the trunk of a car. A child was walking toward her. When she focused on it was not a child; it was Agent Raintree in another of her poor dress choices. Gee, Dana thought I hope Micky's end of the assignment is going better than mine.

"I MUST CONFESS THAT when I heard you were returning, I started filling the room with lawyers."

Ruth Miller explained, leading Micky into her office. The office was plush with large calves, skin leather chairs and enormous mahogany desk. Ruth Miller was a beautiful woman in her late forties. She and a reddish tint to her hair and professional styling.

When she walked, it was clear that she had confidence in herself. Her bright green eyes looked through people.

Still, there was a sadness within her. Some matters had gone differently than she wished for, even with the best planning and preparation.

"But you choose not to."

Micky confirmed.

Ruth opened a bottle of water and handed one to Micky. Micky's policy was never to eat or drink anything a suspect gives you. But he knew he needed her trust. He accepted the water and took a drink.

"Let me start by apologizing for the spat between your partner and me. Some things are hard for a woman to take as she gets a little older. Your partner knew where to land the jabs to hurt me the most. The comment about Vincent cutting me off sent me over the edge."

"So, you two were lovers."

"I loved him, and I still do, but he feels the need to move on."

"When my partner and I were here last, you explained the widget business to me." Now is a good time to test the waters for a bit of truth.

"The worst thing about being involved in clandestine contracting is that you have to lie to people. Friends and family to start with, then you realize you are lying to people that otherwise could have been friends." Ruth smiled at Micky and rested back in her comfortable chair. She had chosen to wear a navy-blue Armani women's business suit. Ruth pushed back from her desk and crossed her eloquent legs slowly, arresting Micky's attention.

"Why don't you start by telling me what you can about what Vincent does for the company? From what I have collected thus far, he doesn't seem like your typical mercenary."

Ruth let out a slight laugh. "Vincent is not a mercenary. Please let me explain. Have you ever seen one of those comedians that can impersonate famous people's voices and sound just like them?"

"Yes, impressionist."

"Well, that is both a gift and a talent. A gift first and talent in that it is something they work to get better at. My dear detective Santiago, my dear Vincent has a knack for languages and speaks fluent Arabic and Farcie, just to name two. But he also can imitate or sound like the regional dialects and infection after he hears the person he is to question."

"So let me get this straight. I speak with a Hispanic accent. Vincent can speak Spanish, and after hearing the regional inflection of the area I come from, he could sound like he grew up next door."

"Correct " also means he can tell when someone is lying about where they were born and raised in the Middle East. He is invaluable."

"So, killing him would only come as a last resort." Micky could feel so many pieces falling into place.

"So now you understand."

"Where does Lisa come in? I mean, she is not his natural daughter. At first, we thought he was keeping her as a sex slave, but the DNA from his bedroom doesn't match her. I will assume if you give me a nod, you feel comfortable assuming it is yours, and we can sidestep any further embarrassment or discussion of that matter."

Ruth nodded her head in affirmation.

"Good, then let's try not to have to touch on that subject again." Micky looked more relieved than Ruth.

"I think this is why I was glad your partner was otherwise engaged. Lisa was his partner's daughter before I met him. Vincent, who had another name at the time, and his partner stayed in a house next door to suspects in a crime. The partner's wife, also working for the government, had a child, and the four were at the house one night, and Vincent went out for pizza. When he came back, the house was in full blaze. Vincent could save Lisa, or whatever her name was then, but not the parents. They were burned alive from what I have been told, and the little girl could hear them screaming."

"That is why she was seeing that doctor."

"Yes LTE, Long term Traumatic Event Syndrome. It is a lot like PTSD. The doctor decided that since Vincent and Lisa were suffering from the same trauma, she would try treating them together. The problem with long-term treatment is that you don't know what the long-term side effects will be. Apparently, one of the lasting side effects was that the two bonded like a real father and daughter, and neither wants to separate the bond."

Micky and another question, but his cell phone rang. He snatched the phone out of his pocket at record speed and answered, then mumbled a few words.

"An emergency?" Ruth guessed.

"Yes, someone is trying to kill my partner again."

"Considering her manners, I bet it happens quite often."

"More than you would think. This is the second time this week."

# Chapter 21

It was a scene that was becoming all too common. There were police and technicians everywhere. The was a barricade of frustrated news people on hand and the site Micky wanted most to see. Dana was walking backward and forward, looking for something on the ground.

"There you are." Dana rushed to recover Jewel, the lucky doll and dust the doll off. The doll had flown from her purse in Dana's mad dash.

"What the hell is that?" Marlow asked as she approached Dana.

"She is sort of a good luck charm loaned to me by a friend."

"Maybe I should send out for a case of rabbit's feet and pass them out to anyone that has to come in contact with you." Marlow prescribed.

"It has nothing to do with luck. Drake saved her reckless ass a second time." Raintree had taken it upon herself to join the scolding.

Raintree and Drake appeared as if waiting for Micky before talking with Dana.

"Look, you guys are clearly ahead of us on this thing. I say we pool our resources and put an end to this mayhem before we all start looking like clowns on the national news." Raintree proposed more directly to Micky than anyone else.

"Look, raggedy Anne, I don't know how you and your giant boyfriend work, but if the only thing you guys have to offer is half-truths and more misdirection, I rather take my chances with the mercenaries." Dana proclaimed.

"Mercenaries?" Marlow asked.

"Yeah, it has something to do with something being proposed by the National Security Council and appearing in Congress soon. Budgetary concerns about how much can be spent on private security firms operating within the US boundaries." Micky added to the conversation.

"Look, buddy, that last statement was a breach of national security. I could have you and your whole outfit arrested and held in federal custody. But we need you, clowns because you have a couple of things; we need to clear up our end of this mess." Raintree stated.

Dana looked closely at Drake.

"Can he talk?"

"Will you please stop picking on him? He keeps saving your butt." Raintree asked.

"I say you four sit down over lunch and decide if you can work together. In the meantime, I have two states prosecutes offices and two governor's offices to lie to about how well we are doing." Marlow snapped. "And what the hell happened to that Lester guy's hand?"

"Well, you know what they say? Eighty percent of accidents happen to twenty percent of the people." Dana reasoned.

"With all due respect to mathematician Pareto, I think it is the twenty percent that have anything to do with you," Raintree added.

THE SMALL GROUP CHOSE the Roadhouse Steakhouse across the street from where Raintree and Drake stayed. Raintree ordered for Drake, and he thanked her. I was not that Drake could not speak, but he felt uncomfortable speaking in groups. During the meal, Drake spilled some sauce on his shirt, and Raintree started wiping it for him. Raintree looked over and saw Dana staring at her. "Oh, really. The two of you? How is that even possible? He must fling you around like a rag doll."

"Is there no limit to the crude things you will say, Besides, our business is just that our business." Raintree smiled at Drake.

"What do you need from us to help you with your end of the investigation?" Micky asked.

"Well, how about the tapes? You see, a little birdie told me he searched the home of one Lester Greer, and there was a series of mini tapes. They were numbered or had names in alphabetical order. Some seemed to be missing, and there were none on the body. I checked when your partner was looking for her good luck charm."

"That sounds fair enough; since they cannot be verified, we give you a copy and no questions about how we obtained the copies," Dana suggested.

"See, we can all get along. Now we want to interview the ground." Raintree suggested.

"The ground?" Micky was surely not familiar with the term.

"Well, dear fellow, that is what those in the undercover business sometimes call the person they is connected to that grounds them to the world. You see, there are agents, not unlike undercover cops, that have fake identification. They are live wires in that at some point their cover could be blown by accident since so much of who they are is made up. So, like any live wire, they need to be grounded to someone that can be checked forward and backward and still proven to be just who they say they are. Like Dr. Rita Reyes. And I think you guys should let us speak to her as a show of good faith."

Drake kept eating while Raintree spoke. From time to time, his eyes would survey the room as if making notes on where everyone in the room was.

"Do take this the wrong way, but you keep talking about what we can give, and you say nothing of what you have to offer," Dana stated, then turned to Drake. "Is she this pushy in private is that how it works?"

Drake put down his fork and looked at Dana as though he was going to say something. They all waited for his comment. He then picked the fork back up and went back to eating. A look of utter frustration came over Dana's face.

"I love it. He is doing that because he knows it throws you off." Micky said in a jovial tone.

"Alright, meet us at the federal lockup this evening, and we let you two speak to our witness. And you consider letting us speak to yours."

"What witness could you possibly have worth our time?" Dana asked.

"I have someone that has worked with those dead mercenaries that are being dropped all over town. She did not work or the current job, but she does have insight into how they operate."

RITA CLICKED OFF ANOTHER round of pictures from the nest she had made. Rita had loaded a backpack with what she thought she would need for her storage locker. It had taken her two days to find where she had been taken the night of Vincent and Barney's abduction. The place looked like an endless string of broken-down abandon homes and businesses.

What made matters far worse, many of the street signs were missing making it hard to retrace her steps. The old bicycle that had faithfully ferried her around campus during her med school days now had a new purpose. She had built a resting place in an abandoned plant with missing sections of the walls.

Rita had been mildly harassed while in the neighborhood but let the would-be predators know she knew the primary rules of predatory behavior. No predator was to attack prey that is stronger or better prepared than them.

She let the fact that she was armed not be a secret. Rita heard a rustling sound from the rooms with multiple broken-out windows behind her. She spun around and pointed her handgun at the sound, and a small dirty-looking dog can out of hiding. The dog had a sad look on its face, and its ribs showed.

"I hope you don't mind if I hang out at your place for a while; some friends of mine are across the way and need help," Rita told the dog, who just stared at her with the saddest eyes she had ever seen.

Rita reached into her backpack and retrieved half of a roast beef sub sandwich she had started earlier. She threw the half-sub to the dog, then retrieved her water bottle and filled a broken bowl she found on the floor for the dog. "Damn." She said as she could see two men in the derelict motel dragging a woman in a mustard-colored suit out of one of the rooms. The woman looked almost lifeless, her hair covering her face, and any resistance to the dragging had subsided.

"Did you see that?"

Rita asked the dog, who said nothing; he just rested on a pile of soggy boxes. Rita took more pictures. "What is your name anyway?" Still, the dog said nothing.

"Pedro. Why don't I call you Pedro? You remind me of my cousin. Only he got more fleas."

Rita began making a map and counting the number of people coming and going from the motel. She scribbled down license numbers and made a note of the type of weapons they were carrying.

"You know Pedro, I hate this spy shit. They give you a shitty little course, and if it wasn't for Barney....."

Before she could complete her complaining, Pedro started a low-pitched growl. "I heard it too she whispered."

Pedro jumped up and ran past her, then returned with a large rat in his mouth. Pedro had crushed the rat's head with his jaws. Pedro dropped the dead rat at Rita's feet, then curled back up on his boxes and continued to survey the room.

"That seems fair. I share my roast beef with you, and you share your rats with me. You might just turn out to be more beneficial than my last boyfriend."

Rita went back to work.

Rita suddenly saw something that might be a game-changer. It was Vincent, and he was walking, not being dragged, and his head was held high.

"There is trouble now, Pedro. Vincent looks like he has a plan."

"ARE YOU A MAN OF HONOR, Cornel?" Vincent asked after entering the office of Cornel Norris.

"Why the question? Do you have something to offer that I might want to take into consideration before the games begin?"

"Cornel, I watched your face as you told the story about the rapping of that man's wife. You never displayed the uncontrollable tells that show in a pervert. That is because you are a soldier, not a monster or pervert. You have held off and given time to us that a viable decision be reached."

The Cornel stood and faced Vincent. "Then how best do we proceed?"

"I have what you want, but I want a couple of things."

"Do you think you are in a position to bargain?"

"I think my position is so weak that you risk nothing by hearing me out and considering the proposal's value."

"Let me guess, you want your life and the life of the others."

"Life by definition is not eternal, nor does it hold any guarantees."

"Now it is you that sounds like the soldier, Mr. Garrison."

"I was told there is upward of ten million dollars of untraceable money in that bank at any given time."

"And you want a piece?"

"Not for myself but for my daughter. She had been traumatized in the past, and she has a chance to go away to school. The money to help her education would be a good use for bad money."

The Cornel paced a little and looked at Vincent, but it was impossible to read him. "How much."

"I would expect you to decide based on what you take in."

"Reasonable. I like that. But you said there were a couple of things. What is the other?"

"The second thing is that too many things have transpired to expect that no one else will die going forward. As I said, life is not eternal. The second thing is that whoever has to die from this point forward dies with their dignity intact."

"Does that include you, Mr. Garrison?"

"Yes, as it does you, Cornel Norris."

"What say I take a couple of hours and think on it."

"As I would expect."

As Vincent was being led back to his captivity, Norris stopped him for one last comment.

"You know guys like you are waste in those think tanks. You would have made a hell of a field commander."

"And all I want is to be a good father to one scared little girl."

# Chapter 22

Two tall guards led the prisoner into the interrogation room. The guards were almost as tall as Drake, but neither had his muscular build. Drake and Raintree stood facing the small black woman that had been led into the room. The black women's hair was a wild mess, and there were burns on one side of her face.

"Victoria, meet Detectives Bullworth and Santiago." Raintree introduced. The guards assisted Victoria into a seat at a metal table where her hands were bound in front of her before they would leave the room.

"You got a smoke?" Victoria asked Raintree.

"I told you before I don't smoke. It's bad for you." Raintree answered.

Dana reached into her pocket, pulled out a fresh pack of cigarettes, and opened them. She handed one to Victoria, then laid the pack in front of her. "You keep them."

Micky leaned over, lit the cigarette for Victoria, and stood in the corner away from her. Victoria took a deep drag of the cigarette, knowing everyone was waiting for her following words. "You see, short bitch that's the difference between street cops and feds. It's called respect. She doesn't smoke either; look how white her fingertips are, but she knew, as a gesture of respect, she would be ready if I asked. And the man cop lit the cigarette and then stepped out of my face. More respect.

You just don't get it do you?"

Micky put pictures of the men that had died over the past days of the operation that had gone haywire. Victoria stated, going through the pictures. "Damn, Drake, what did you use on this guy? A bazooka."

Dana tried to hide her surprise that it appeared that the woman in custody not only knew Drake but could recognize his work. "So, I guess you guys want to know who hires guys like this." Victoria guessed.

" If you tell us, you could be out of here before your three-year-old turns her first trick." Raintree's comment put matching looks of disdain on the faces of Dana and Micky.

"Look, I'm out of here. I want to catch the bad guy as much as the next girl, but I can't put someone's kid on the block." Dana stood up and looked over at Micky, who was also preparing to leave.

"Well, I be God Damn, you don't know who you hooked up with. Don't leave just yet; let me explain." Victoria's proclamation stopped Dana and Micky in their tracks. "What did Agent Raintree tell you Drake was. Just another federal agent. That's class A bullshit. Drake is a killer. The government uses him and about ten others like him to eradicate people when there is a major government fuck up." Victoria smiled at Drake. "You know, I used to think stories about government assassins were fairy tales. They told us boots to keep us in line after we learned the trade. That was until I saw what one of you robots did to Major Riggins."

"I'm starting to think this was a bad idea." Raintree interrupted.

Something in what Victoria was saying started to make sense to Dana and Micky. "Look, it works like this say you have a former Seal Team leader who goes ape shit. The man is not only a trained killer. Hell, he trains killers. Not to mention the fucker knows where all the bodies are buried. You need a guy that is a super killer to take him out."

"You are oversimplifying Victoria." Raintree tried to redirect.

"Yeah, well over, simplification or not, my ass is safer in here."

"I need this guy, Victoria; who is he?" Dana asked as if she and Victoria were the only two in the room.

"Answer her question, and I will sign the patrician to have your daughter removed from child services and placed with her grandmother," Raintree stated.

"I'm holding you to her keeping her word cop," Victoria told Dana. "The man you are looking for is called Cornel Norris. He was hired for a mission inside the states, and that is rare as hen's teeth."

"What was the mission?" Raintree asked.

"Thank you, Victoria," Dana said, concluding the conversation. There was nothing else she wanted to say, and Victoria got the message.

"HOW DO I KNOW YOU ARE giving me copies of all the tapes?" Raintree ask after the foursome had exited the federal lockup in downtown St. Louis.

"It's not all, and I am telling you that upfront. It would appear one of the techniques our boy Lester had for collecting information that no other reporter could get was seducing underage girls and taking them all the way, shall we say."

"Oh my."

"If the news people come for my head for putting him in danger or if they decide to go after the police department, I want something I can use that may be heard in closed judge's chambers that will provide me some ammunition."

"I see, so that sounds like a separate case, not part of my investigation or federal on the face of it. So, I will give you that." Raintree concluded.

"Tell me one thing would you use a three-year-old as bait to make a point?"

Micky asked.

"Grow up, Santiago; this is the big leagues." In her ill-fitting suit, Raintree took Drake by the hand and led him off.

"Dana, I need you to promise me one thing," Micky stated as the federal agents left.

"What's that?"

"That no matter how mad you get at how things are unfolding; you will keep your mind on the objective. We are now much closer to fixing things and cannot afford to go backward."

Dana felt a little embarrassed that Micky had read the anger in her face and knew how self-destructive she could be at times. "Deal. Now promise me one thing."

"Anything, partner."

"I would never tell you how to treat your daughters but consider that right now a little forgiveness would go a long way with Maria. I won't pretend to know how it hurts you to see her caught in a mess that she could have avoided following what you and her aunt have been teaching her all her life. But Micky, please don't let her mistake change the way the two of you look at each other from now on. Take it from someone raised by the shittyist possible parent."

DANA AND MICKY DROVE to the police station but found that with the death of a member of the new community, even the national news people now wanted a piece of the action and were camped out all over the area. They decided to go to Micky's house to regroup. Micky had promised to take Dana to her apartment to see if her landlord had calmed down and would let Dana move back in.

"Why don't we take a walk and have a little father-daughter talk," Micky suggested to Maria. When Micky and Dana entered the house, Micky noticed his daughter trying to avoid eye contact. Micky led her out the back through the kitchen door. Rosa, Micky's sister, a portly woman with a plain face, was watching a cooking show in the kitchen with Isabella. Isabella bolted toward Dana the minute she saw her and hugged her. "Did Jewel give you good luck today?" Burst from Isabella.

"Boy, did she. I want to hold on to her for a few more days if you don't mind."

"She will keep you safe and bring you home every night."

Dana looked up to notice Rosa staring at her. "I moved your things to my brother's room. I hope you are comfortable there."

"Whoa, slow down. Did you talk to your brother about that?"

Rosa now stared like she had seen a ghost. "Ma'am, my brother is a man of honor."

Just then, a cell phone rang, and Dana went to answer it but realized it was Micky's phone. He had laid it down when he went to talk to Maria.

"I must have the worst communication skills in town." Dana picked up the phone. "Bullworth, Detective Santiago is busy at the moment. Can I give him a message?"

"Are you two close?" A Hispanic woman asked on the other end of the phone. Is this a relative or a former or current love? She began to wonder.

What does she mean by close? These were the thoughts that rocketed through her mind. "He is my partner. We work together."

There was a pause. "Tell your partner to check his email."

"I MADE A DEAL WITH the cornel," Vincent announced to his fellow prisoners when they were alone again.

"What kind of deal?" Barney asked.

"I am going to tell them where the bank is in exchange for some of the money."

"That is stupid; he is going to kill us the minute you tell him?" Doctor Walker stated. She was still shaking from her interview with the madman.

"It is dumber than you think. He has no idea where the bank is; only I do." Marta told Walker.

"So, you plan to sell them smoke. That way, they have to keep someone alive until the site is verified."

"It is really a good plan, except the part where I die." Barney chuckled.

"That's preposterous. The only one they will surely live is her, and she won't tell you where the freaking location is."

"But it gives her a fighting chance to complete her mission." Coldly Vincent stated in response to Walker's anger.

"Look, Vincent, what about Lisa?" Walker asked.

"She was going away to school in the fall. I may have taken her as far as a parent can. God, I love my baby, but I have an obligation to you and this country."

"Barney, tell him he's losing his mind. I have worked with criminally insane people before. That colonel guy is the real deal." Walker pleaded with Barney.

"It's his call. Life has been nice, but without Serena, maybe it's all for the best." Barney's jovial mask started dropping, and he was again descending into a hell of eternal separation from a lover.

"Look, lady, I don't know who you are or who you represent, but I don't want to die.

I just don't want to die." Walker broke down into tears.

"I need you to hold out as long as you can. Rita from my team is not a spy, but she is a support person. She has had a course on how to react. There is a chance she will rescue you after we leave." Vincent spoke in a soft voice then when in a dark corner of the room to pray.

"You are no doubt the leader of your team," Marta called into the darkness, where Vincent conversed with his maker. "You see, I am also a team leader. Or at least I was. Jacob had no fear of death; he had lived a long time in a game where men die every day.

But Mosses. Poor sweet Mosses." She paused for a moment. "I met his father and mother once. They were so proud to have a son who graduated from West Point, no affirmative action bullshit, a real cadet. Their family had a long tradition of service to this country. He was the crown jewel of their achievement. And those bastards killed him. Team leader, what if I tell you where the location is?" Marta asked.

"Then it may increase our chances of staying alive," Walker stated in a trembling voice.

"While exponentially increasing the cornel's chance of slipping away," Barney added.

"There is no way I let you people risk dying while dealing me out to save my life." Marta proclaimed.

A SMALL GROUP ASSEMBLED in one of the conference rooms at the police headquarters. Dana and Micky had been forced to push into the station through a pack of news crews.

The news people were not only demanding answers, but many seemed to be making up their own. All through the entry to the station Micky kept his arm locked with Dana. Micky knew she was far more easily baited by bad behavior, and they could not afford a setback.

"Whoever your man on the ground is, he just saved a bunch of lives." Donavan, the SWAT commander that had been asked to join the meeting, assessed. Dr. Reyes had sent 28 pictures, a couple of hand-drawn diagrams, and a listing of weapons she could recognize.

"How so? Lt Malow asked.

"Well, the weapons an entry team usually carries are light. We need to move fast and stay agile. Some of the stuff he spotted as weapons would have clearly given them the firepower advantage when and if all hell broke loose."

"She." Dana corrects. "Dr. Reyes." Dana jumped to her feet. The picture that had been sent to Mickey's email had been made into a

PowerPoint by Sonya from the police IT team, and Sonya was flashing through the photo on a large screen in front of the group.

"That's him," Dana screamed. "That our man among the missing. As of this time yesterday, he is still alive and awaiting rescue.

"Where the hell are they? Those pictures look like Bruit or downtown Fallujah."

Marlow asked.

"No such luck. You see the trash. Every country has its own garbage. It's like the old saying that one man's leftovers is another man's feast. That is good old USA trash." Clarkson commented.

Clarkson was a Detective that was beyond retirement age. He had held several posts in his over thirty-year career. Now he works mainly as an advisor using his history as a guide and resource.

"Nowhere here does she show the structure's name or street signs," Donovan commented.

"I haven't met a doctor who wasn't a freak for taking notes. I wonder how she missed that in these many pictures." Marlow commented.

"We don't think she missed it. We think she is leaving certain things out on purpose." Dana commented.

"Why?" Captain Maynard, a mean-looking man in a decorated police uniform, asked in a stern voice. Maynard was the leader of police intelligence.

"Sir, we strongly believe at this time she feels her team was set up by someone with active knowledge of their operations. So, she feels she needs us as outsiders to commence the rescue." Micky explained.

"So, at best, she thinks she has a rat; at worst, she thinks she has a mole," Maynard noted with a wide-eyed stare at the PowerPoint slides being displayed. "Where is the FBI in all this I thought you were working together?"

"It would appear that they have been working overtime to shoot the people trying to shoot my detectives," Marlow answered.

"Sounds like a worthwhile pursuit." Clarkson chuckled and winked at Dana.

"MICKY, I THINK IT IS time I check out of your house and find a hotel room."

Dana announced after the meeting.

The remainder of the meeting went well. Dana was returning her service weapon to full duty, not that she and exactly left it.

"Is it the food? Because if it's a little too spicy. I can have my sister tone it down." Micky asked, organizing the papers on his desk.

"No, Micky, the food is great. Your sister is an excellent cook." Dana worked at her desk, trying to hide her expression from Micky.

"Then is it something the girls have done?"

"No, Micky, I think you know how much I love the girls. They help me feel like a real person, not just residual rage from a bad upbringing."

"Then that only leaves me." Micky put down the papers to give her his full attention. "Is there something I have done or not done that is causing you to want to run to a new residence when the case we are working on continues to heat up."

"Slow down, Micky. Your sister saw me leaving your bedroom this morning and assumed certain things. She said she is moving my things to your room."

Dana could saw a talk Black man that looked familiar wandering about the detective squad room like a kid at his first time at Disneyland. She could not place him. He wore jeans and a Lakers jacket and looked tall and athletic enough to be a Laker.

"Dana, I understand you did not want me to think that you and my sister are conspiring. The truth is she knows how much the girls love you, and she has always been more than a little concerned that I would take up with some woman that the girls hate, or that wanted her out of the house."

Dana and Micky looked at each other both a little embarrassed, then finally, Micky stated. "Now that we have that cleared up and you are staying for the time being, let's go see what Jerome wants."

Jerome, Officer Roberto Reyes's partner. Dana had missed it because he looked so different in street clothes.

"You know everyone wants to work up here but to tell the truth, it doesn't look that much better than where we work." Jerome assessed, and Dana and Micky approached.

"You have a message from Dr. Reyes for us," Micky stated.

"I guess that's why you guys make the big money. She says your target is in Washington Park." Jerome's message seemed to drain all the blood from Micky's face. Micky turned around, searching for someone. It needed to be clarified to Dana or Jerome he needed. "Tell me something, how come when you see spies in the movies that have Faris and Lamborghini, and you got the sister peddling around on a Schwinn?"

Micky spotted Donavan, the SWAT commander, and ran to him with Dana and Jerome on his heels. "Donavan, if the target is in Washington Park on the other side of the river, how does that change the takedown."

Mikey's question knocked the wind out of Donavan. "Micky, St. Louis has a little over one thousand sworn police officers.

East. St. Louis has sixty-six.

Washington Park has 6. Against twenty or so highly trained mercenaries with fully automatic weapons and body armor, it would be a ......."

"Bloodbath," Jerome stated.

"Do you see it? The person setting up this jacked-up operation knew that going in.

They stacked the deck." Dana explained.

"Well, the way it works, my authority stops at the county line unless the St. Louis City cops invite me in, but my authority and theirs end halfway over on the bridge. We cannot invade another state. If we could get convenience your FBI playmates to let up and assist them rather than waiting for their own SWAT team, we can go in."

"That is still going to piss a lot of people off," Micky said. "But we have no choice. Now we wait for Rita to call Roberto. Then Roberto calls Jerome here, and we know the location." Micky explained.

"Damn, man, you really are a detective," Jerome mumbled.

# Chapter 23

The door to the cell opened slowly, and there stood Cornel Norris. The expression on his face as coarse as the three-day stubble of his salt and pepper beard, looked as if he was at the end of his resolve.

The outer reaches of his patience had been breached.

"I agree to your terms, Mr. Garrison, but I will accept no foolishness and no betrayal.

You and the woman from the cleaners will go with us to the point where the bank is. When we have taken down the bank, I will call the troops I leave behind, and your associate and Doctor Walker can walk home from here."

"Hey Vincent, can we trust this guy?" Barney called out.

"Don't you see it, Barney? He got locked into this mess like we did by the same person."

Vincent's statement seemed to seal the deal for the Cornel. The Cornel now knew the unspoken aspects of the relationship between all involved in the busted play was known to Vincent. Now Vincent, even trapped and bound, was like a genie in a bottle. Releasing him to some degree might mean the Cornel and his men could not only leave this hellish place but leave rich.

Three large vehicles exited the motel and drove to the main street of Bond and started toward the direction of St. Louis with Vincent and Marta seated wedged between armed men. The driver of the last vehicle slammed on his brakes to miss a dog the was crossing the street. What looked like an old homeless woman screamed out. "Damn fool, don't hit my dog; you suppose to have more sense than him."

The woman crossed in front of the car, dropped something, then reached down, pulled something from her bag, and attached it to the underside of the front bumper. It was a prepaid cell phone turned on and taped to a magnet.

"Get the fuck out of the street, old bitch." The driver shouted.

The old woman, who just happened to be Dr. Rita Reyes in disguise, got out of the street and headed back to her hiding nest. "Some people have no manners at all, Pedro."

Pedro said nothing.

DANA KNOCKED ON THE hotel door where Raintree was staying, and it took a while, but Agent Raintree finally made it to the door. Raintree opened the door slightly more than a crack. Raintree's hair was a mess, and her makeup was smeared.

"Look, this is not a good time." Raintree began as Dana pushed the door open and barged in. Drake just had time to grab a pillow to hind his nakedness and dash into the bathroom. Both Dana and Micky's eyes looked like they were going to explode.

Raintree was wearing a kimono that drooped over her boyish frame.

"Now we are two consenting adults."

"I don't care." Dana cut Raintree off. "We got the call from Reyes, and we are ramping up to go in and bring the kidnap victims out."

"Then, nothing you saw here will appear in any report. Is that correct?"

"Agent Raintree, let me tell you a little about how I work. When I fill out an official police report, I often have to tell a little white lie or two. But if I were to write a report that says Superman there gets a major hard-on for ragamuffins, no one would believe anything else I write down ever again." Dana stopped and shook her head as if trying to get a visual out of her mind.

"Now the village where they are being held has a police force of six full-time and 12 part-time officers. We need the FBI to lead us in because it is on the Illinois side of the river."

"Oh. I can do that, but I will need to inform the Illinois state police that we are going in, and they can assist. Otherwise, you will have arrest warrant issues up the yen yang.

PEDRO DROPPED A THIRD dead rat in front of Rita's nest in the abandoned building, and she gave him another roast beet sub sandwich. "It seems so unfair you keep bringing me rats, and I haven't eaten my first." Pero looked at Rita with his sad eyes, but now there seemed to be gratitude glowing on the fringes. "I have to go and meet the Calvary; they will be here soon, the place is going to get pretty noisy, and you might want to hide and protect your doggy ears." Pedro went and sat in his favorite watching position. "With any luck, this is our last day as secret agents, and I can go back to being a doctor, and you can go back to whatever it is you do. Now let's pray that all the potholes in this raggedy place don't knock the cell phone off the vehicle."

"WELL, IT'S ABOUT TIME," Rita told Donavan as he stepped from the led vehicle.

A convoy of police vehicles converged at the gas station a little more than two blocks from the motel.

Rita ran to the man she could tell was running the show.

"Are you Doctor Reyes?" Donavan asked.

"Yes."

"Thank you for your intel; we are on our way in to get your friends out safe and sound."

People were getting out of vehicles and surrounding Rita they wanted to hear firsthand what she had to offer.

"Change of plans. Vincent and the woman calling herself Marta are in the vehicle with a man calling himself Cornel Norris. They are headed to an unknow site in St. Louis."

"Damn." Donavan exclaimed.

"Okay so here is the play. I attached a live cell phone to one of the vehicles. I can give you the number and you can triangulate the location. I already sent you the license plate number. In the meantime, Barney and Doctor Walker need to be rescued from the motel.

No doubt when those bastards get whatever it is they want from Vincent they will kill the hostages."

"Alright team you heard the lady. New plan. We split the team. Captain you and Lt Marlow led the blue team back into the city, waited for the location then move in. We have Illinois State police coming in from the west to reinforce so let's just hope we have enough bodies to keep the drama down. Detectives you will remain here until we secure the area."

Drake turned to Raintree who stood there listening to Rita. "You stay here with the detectives." he said in a dry voice.

"My job." Raintree started to say.

"Please."

"Alright but you be careful." Raintree conceded.

"I guess he can talk." Dana mumbled to Micky.

"Just hold on to Jewel I think we are still going to need her luck."

After the snipers had been put into place, a lead police car, with its lights flashing, drove toward the front of the motel. The driver stopped the car and pulled out a megaphone.

"Unauthorized occupants of this structure, this the police you are under arrest, please lay down any weapons you might have and exit with your hands above your head." However, the eloquence nor the content of the officer's speech stopped the two mercenaries the front of the entrance from opening fire. In a fraction of a second, the police car was perforated, and the officer fell backward. A sniper shot one of the mercenaries with a clear head shot, and the other ducked back into the opening of the motel.

"Runner, you're up." Donavan slapped the back of a police officer wearing a backpack. The officer was a young thin man who looked built for running. He took off with starting block acceleration and dashed toward the opening, jumping and hurdling obstructions, then diving over a railing. The runner made a spin move, followed by a football field jut jut moved to duck gunfire, and he bounded to the side of one of the parked vehicles in the courtyard. The runner slid to a stop, assessed the angles he was being fired upon in a fraction of a second then proceeded. A mercenary shot out the windows of one of their vehicles, trying to hit the runner, but it was useless.

In the meantime, officers and snipers lay down cover fire for the runner, but it was not the shooting of the mercenaries that were wandering about the courtyard that was the main issue. Rita had mentioned in her report that there was a M240b on the second level of the motel. A M240B is a 950-round-per-minute bandelier-fed machine gun that usually carries an armor-piercing 7.62 NATO round. This weapon is frequently used to take out handheld machine guns. The very weapon that concerned the SWAT team most. The runner found Door 26c, the room where he was told by Rita the hostages were. The runner shot the lock and the hinges, then hit the door with his shoulder. He burst into the room to find Barney and Doctor Walker huddled together in the room. The runner pointed his gun at Barney. "Last four of your social security number."

"What?" Dazed, Barney asked.

"Tell me the last four numbers of your social security number, or I shoot you."

"1701." Barney answered, and without being asked, Dr. Walker volunteered hers. Dr Walker then made a move toward the door.

"No, that's not the way out. They would have closed the courtyard by now."

The runner restrained her. He then entered the bathroom and began setting explosive charges on the wall. The red head buzz cut merch ran into the room with her weapon drawn and pointed it at the back of the runner. Barney grabbed her, and she lost her primary weapon but pulled her killing knife from its sheaf. Barney grabbed the buzz-cuts woman's wrist and twisted it. He shoved the blade of the knife up under the woman's ribs and twisted. It was the same move used to kill his poor Serena. Barney then looked into Buzz's Cuts eyes and turned the blade, and kissed her slightly. "That is for Serena." Barney watched the light go out in Buzz Cuts eyes, and a part of him relaxed.

"Are you sure you guys are a lost interpreter team?" The runner asked as he witnessed Barney kill the woman. "If we make it out of here alive, we have got to sit down over a beer, and you can explain how a bunch of support nerds get in shit this deep. In the meantime." The runner paused and then yelled. "Fire in the hole."

The runner ducked, as did Barney and the doctor. A huge explosion blew through the cinderblock wall into a muddy field in the back. Without fanfare, the runner grabbed the doctor and shoved her through the hole while kicking out a loose cinder block. Two officers grabbed her and assisted on the other side of the hole. Soon Barney and the runner were clear of the cell.

"Runner reporting. We are clear. Repeat clear to engage. We have rescue complete."

Drake walked deliberately to his car's trunk and loaded an AV-140 MSGL - 40mm Multi-Shot Grenade Launcher from the trunk and loaded it. The launcher shot a red stream that was little more than a flash until it hit the machine gun barricade where the M240b was. The grenade set off the stockpile of ammunition and blasted with an explosion that was more significant than any ten fireworks burst ever seen in the heavens.

This blast sent smoke, fire, and human body parts sailing through the air. All the car alarms on the vehicles in the courtyard went off simultaneously.

And a spray of glass blasted, covering the entire area. There was a cracking sound as the section of the second floor gave way and plummeted into a burning pile. The smell of cordite and smoke now replaced the foul mold and junkyard smell. There was no need to wonder about the merc that had run to fire the M240b. The would-be gunner was undoubtedly incinerated by the grenade blast of Drake or crushed by falling cinderblocks. The building shook, and the ground started to rumble. A fire trunk could be heard a short distance away, as could the lonesome hobo call of a train. The fire trunk may have been stuck behind the train, but it did not matter. Nothing the police wanted to save at his point was in jeopardy.

Groups of SWAT officers with battering rams knocked down all the doors to the motel and were assisted by the State Troopers. They dragged out the occupants and laid them face down in the courtyard.

Resistance was met with force and resilience.

After the mercenaries accepted the futility of skirmishes, they were rounded up, and the Illinois state trooper read them their rights. The commander signaled, and the group left at the gas station to join the tactical team.

"Barney, I did remember everything you taught me." Rita rushed to Barney, who was being cared for on a stretcher.

"You must be Barney, and this must be Doctor Walker," Dana affirmed, walking up with Micky. "We have a bunch of questions for you guys as soon as the paramedics say it's okay."

"That's going to have to wait, ma'am." A state trooper ran up to Dana and Micky.

"We just got word that they found the vehicles we were tracking; they are stopped outside a liquor store on your side of the water. That makes it your problem. I am told to get you guys and the FBI on the scene as soon as possible."

"You do know St. Louis is the other way?" Dana asked as Dana and Micky rushed in a patrol car that was being followed by the car carrying Raintree and Drake. "Last time I check, ma'am, but Frank Holden State Park is right there." As the trooper pulled to a stop, they could all see a helicopter preparing to land in the softball field. There was the thundering beat of the powerful motor and the draft caused by the whirling blades.

"You aren't going to tell me you are one of those winey women that are afraid of a little helicopter, are you?" The trouper mocked.

"Baby, I am the kind of woman that eats bitches like that for breakfast," Dana answered.

"Young man, I have also seen her make a snack out of a trooper or two. A word to the wise, you might say." Micky added.

# Chapter 24

Boldly Cornel Norris and his soldiers walked into the Cut-Rate liquor store. They were led by Vincent and Marta. Vincent and Marta's hands were still bound. An old man rang up a customer, saw Norris's group entering, and pulled out a small pistol. A machine gun fire and shatter the small traveler liquor bottle on the shelf behind the old man by passing bullets through his body.

There were at least a dozen people shopping at the store. Half were at the register waiting to be checked out, and the other half were still making their selection. They all froze at the gunshots.

"Cornel, they are in your way," Vincent said. "Too many to watch and hope they don't do something stupid. They are a distraction and offer no value. Securing them and watching them will slow you down from emptying the content you came for."

There was an undeniable flood of logic to what Vincent said, and the Cornel knew it. This type of raid was different from what he was used to. "Alright, if you are a customer, get whatever you came for and leave. Don't worry about stopping by the checkout." Norris instructed. Then he looked at a rail-thin, dark-complected man behind the counter.

"Take me to the bank."

"The bank is across the street." The man said in an overly projected accent, pretending not to understand the order. Norris grabbed an older woman who was likely one of the store owners. Norris slapped her hard, and she sailed over a rack of snack cakes.

"Let's start by stripping this old bitch down and seeing what makes her tick."

"There is no further need for your display of brutal hostility. I will give you what you want." A calm voice came from a man who appeared in a fez and an old worn suit. "Follow me."

Behind a false wall in the storeroom was the room known as the bank. There was a safe. It was open; there was counting going on, and there were millions of dollars in used bills in stacks. There was a wide variety of photography equipment and copiers. But what caught Vincent's eye was that a couple of machines had no doubt been stolen from the US government and the Department of Motor Vehicles. The equipment for making driver's licenses and passports was there. They would be indistinguishable from the real thing because they were the real thing for all practical intent and purposes. These things, Vincent thought. They are the mission within a mission. Unnoticeable to the colonel and his men, Marta flashed Vincent a slight look. Vincent saw what she found of great importance. The was a pile of half-finished documents and pictures. How easy it had been for those of ill will to the United States to wander into a busy midwestern liquor store, then walk out with a totally new identity. An identity that would allow them to fly anywhere in the country and intermingle with the rest of the citizenry. Waiting for instructions to activate their designated plan. This was what Marta saw as not only more critical than Vincent and the lives of his teammates but also her life. This part of the operation posed a far greater threat to national security than the money. The Cornel snapped out of the wide-eyed wonderment he was joined by one of his men running into the room.

"Sir, the place is surrounded by police, and there appears to be a SWAT unit out there.

The Cornel pulled out his model 1911-.45 caliber automatic and pointed it at Vincent's face. "Remember that death with your dignity intact."

"You don't want to pull that trigger until you hear what I have to say."

"You screwed me." The Cornel uttered through clenched teeth.

"You got screwed, alright, but it wasn't me. If I screwed you, I would be outside, and you would be here."

Now the Cornel was listening. Marta stood there perplexed. The man with the gun pointed at Vincent's face and seemed to be yielding power to Vincent.

"Who?"

"Who could set up a series of what appeared to be random fuck ups and make a mission out of it. Better still. I will give you an easy one. I have never touched Doctor Walker. But someone told you we were lovers." Vincent smiled. "Who?"

"That sneaky conniving bitch." The Cornel screamed as reality hit him hard. "This is all because you dump her?"

"Now I am confused," Marta said, not bothering to use her fake accent.

"Where is your accent?" The Cornel asked.

"What difference could it possibly make? In a couple of minutes, the SWAT guy is going be blowing holes in the roof and swinging in on ropes. Shit, we are probably just as dead as you." Marta commented.

"Leave." The Cornel instructed.

"What?" Vincent asked.

"Remember the promise of death with dignity. I need you to lead my men out with their heads held high. This was my failure to see the treachery in your former lover. I should have thought that her rejection caused her to put you in harm's way by alternating small pieces of the information she gave me. It is no reflection on their ability to carry out orders."

After Vincent and Marta had left the room, but before they had exited the store, they heard the single .45 caliber gunshot that was the cornels death with dignity intact.

"You must be Vincent Garrison. I have been dying to meet you. One parent to another." Micky rushed up, releasing the bonds from Vincent's wrist.

"Single parenthood is much harder." Vincent joked.

"Especially with a daughter the bites?" Dana added.

"Good to have you back in the fold, ma'am," Raintree said, releasing Marta's bonds.

"Where is the giant boyfriend of yours?" Marta asked.

"He said he had some adjusting to do," Raintree answered.

"There are some machines and some documents you need to secure in a room where you will find the body of Cornel Norris. There is also a shit load of cash; secure that two." Marta instructed Raintree.

"Your team is at the hospital, and we are taking you there. Would it be alright with you if we stop by and tell your daughter we have you safe and sound?"

Dana asked, and Vincent's smile gave the answer.

LISA HELD HER SOPHISTICATED teen composure for only a moment, then broke down and cried like a baby to hear her father had been found. "I know I can be such a baby when it comes to my dad, but most parents have little choice. He chose not to abandon me. He taught me things like the phone codes in case I got in trouble and how to use a gun."

"He told us to tell you his abduction in no way lets you and Alexis off the hook for your next cooking lesson. It is on something called Chicken Cacciatore, and it sounds delicious."

Micky added.

Lisa held her hand to her face to hold back the tears of joy. "Will you come and join us for dinner when we make it? And bring your daughters?"

"I would not miss it for the world," Micky answered.

"Will you come too, Detective Bullworth?" Lisa asked.

"Only if you promise to bite only the chicken and not me."

"Deal," Lisa answered with release invading her face.

The type of news delivery made Dana and Micky remember why they did this job.

# Chapter 25

"Isabella said she saw you getting out of a helicopter on the news," Maria shouted as Dana and Micky returned home.

Maria, Isabella, and Rosa charged Dana and Micky as if they had returned from a great war.

"Alright, family, now hear this. Ms. Bullock is moving in with us for the time being. Are there any objections?" Micky announced, watching the smiling faces surrounding him. "Now that's settled."

"Where would you like for me to place your things, Ms. Dana? Rosa asked politely."

'Wherever your brother would like for them to be. He is, after all, head of the household."

"Ms. Dana, you are just in time for hair washing," Isabella announced.

"Lead the way."

DANA WALKED INTO THE office of Ruth Miller. Detective Spooner had called them to the scene. The body of Miller lye on the floor of her office.

"When I checked the sign-in logs, I saw you guys have visited the deceased recently. Thought maybe you might have some insights into how she came to be dead." Spooner was a large Black Detective with a boyish face.

"What was the method of the homicide?" Dana asked.

"It was what used to be called an adjustment. The person is grabbed from behind by the lower jaw, and an upward motion causes the person's body weight to dislocate the vertebrae. A lot like the way they wring chicken's necks. The only thing is that with a human, the person adjusting would be strong and tall. Sound like anybody you two know?"

"Not me," Micky said, turning to Dana. "How about you."

"No one comes to mind off the top of my head.

# End

JUST AS IT HAS BEEN the duty of lighthouses for hundreds of years to guide ships safely into harbors. Thank you for allowing us at the Looking Glass Lighthouse to steer your thoughts dreams and imagination safely to a port of enjoyment.

We are pleased that you have chosen to join us on this journey.

Please feel free to send feedback, questions, and comments to Lookingglasslighthouse@gmail.com and be sure to make your preferred literature vendor aware of your experience.

As a special thank you for allowing us to entertain you we would like to give you a special sneak peek into a due to be released soon work by Alex Mitchell. Man Among the Missing

# Chapter 1

The regal bone structure of the Congress Hotel flaunted the Majestic Grandeur of the aged facility. She stood 28 stories tall and was the product of countless renovations and fittings. The main lobby had a large open area with grey marble tile. The tile led to the check-in desk. From this view, you could see a water fountain in the lobby.

The rooms from the main structure were of atrium configuration. Guest rooms from the second floor to the 28th circled the atrium, and a large hollow area led upward to a stained-glass roof. A red rod iron railing on all the floors surrounding the atrium kept anything or anyone from being pushed or dropped off the center and descending onto the lobby's center.

Ramona and Lizzy stood reconciling the receipts.

The reconciliation in a hotel is done in the middle of the night. All the cash registers from all over the Hotel are balanced to account for every penny taken in. Gift shops, bars, and restaurants must match the revenue collected.

"No matter how much of that nasty coffee you pour me, I aint waking up any faster," Lizzy remarked to Ramona as Ramona poured more coffee into Lizzy's cup. Both women were young recent graduates from a hotel-motel management program. Ramona was an unremarkable-looking black girl aspiring to climb the corporate ladder oozing from every pore.

Lizzy was a plain-looking redhead girl with a pale complexion and glass that looked three sizes too large for her face.

"Why do they give access to cash registers to so many people that just can't count?" Lizzy commented.

"I wish they were stealing. At least we could have them fired." Ramona remarked.

"I think it's in the Constitution that you cannot fire someone for being stupid."

Suddenly a loud crash and splashing sound came from the direction of the lobby. Ramona and Lizzy sat briefly in the small office behind the reservation desk staring wide-eyed at each other.

"Oh God, what was that?" Lizzy was first to exclaim though the sentiment was mutual.

"We go look together." Ramona rationalized.

The women creep too slowly with their arms interlocked to the desk. There in the center of the hotel fountain was the source of the loud noise. A buxom blonde girl lye wearing only a baby doll nighty top, and Her head was wrenched into a contorted position, showing she was dead.

Her crystal blue eyes stared out toward Ramona and Lizzy. Whatever this woman's eyes wanted to convey was now eternally lost to this world. The dyed blue water from the fountain continued to pump, and slowly, the blue of the water became red and overflowed onto the lobby floor.

Ramona and Lizzy heard a stirring and muffled conversation. They looked up. On the 9th floor, at the railing, was a circle of faces of guests in various stages of shock and disbelief. When the guest saw that Ramona and Lizzy noticed them, the faces disappeared, and the unmissable rustle of mass packing began.

"We had better call the cops." Lizzy offered.

"Bullshit, we had better call the resident. He can call the cops."

"Mr. Wakefield, maybe you can explain the laps between when your staff discovered the body and when it was reported."

Detective Blake asked. In many hotels, there is a resident manager. This manager usually lives on the hotel property and is responsible when things happen at odd hours.

Detective Blake, an athlete-looking man in his mid-thirties, had convinced the small group into the office behind the reservations desk. The group consisted of Ramona and Lizzy, as well as Detective Yolanda Carter, Detective Blakes's partner, and two uniformed officers that had been the first to respond to the call. Hiram Wakefield was a thin-paste complexion man with an oversized Adam's apple protruding from his throat. Mr. Wakefield appeared still in shock over the discovery. He sweated profusely and consumed more than his share of the small room oxygen.

"Look, I have contacted the legal rep for the Hotel, and he should be here shortly. Until he arrives, I don't think it would be wise to answer any questions."

Wakefield offered in a shaky voice.

"Look, dick face; no one is trying to get you to confess. We have some general questions to help us categorize the event." Detective Carter noted, eyeing the group. Carter's stare rested on Ramona, and Ramona defiantly returned the gaze. "Let's do an easy question, what are the dead girls' names?'

"How would I know?" Wakefield answered.

"Don't you get the names of your guest?" Blake asked.

"I never said she is or was a guest."

"Oh, Hiram, please don't try to tell me some blonde double D wanders in off the street and walks up to the front desk and says, excuse me, I seem to have lost my underpants. Can you help me find them?"

At this point, the uniformed officers, who had been virtually unnoticed, began chucking at Detective Carter's actions.

"Nine. She came from the ninth floor." Ramona answered.

Hiram Wakefield pointed a long bony finger at Ramona.

"You could be fired for giving out information on a guest."

"Sir, if you fire her for cooperating with an authorized official, she can sue the Hotel. The Hotel would have no choice but to sue you for mismanagement and misrepresentation." Blake informed Wakefield.

"That's right, Hiram baby, she could have you sued out of your jockey shorts. Not that you will need them because if you keep obstructing an active investigation, you could end up in jail playing every night is date night with the brothers in a small romantic prison cell." Carter gave Wakefield a wink that seemed to dissolve the last of his resolves.

"Sounds like it's time to round up everyone on the ninth floor for some questions," Blake announced to one of the uniformed officers.

"You can't," Lizzy said in a small voice. She had been almost totally hidden behind Ramona.

"And why the hell not?" Carter asked in a loud voice.

"Because they all checked out," Lizzy answered.

Blake and Carter turned and stared at Wakefield, totally speechless.

"Cuff this son of a bitch and read him his rights."

These where the first words Carter was able to form.

# And just in case you have not yet had time to find out about the Shepherds Pass Series here is a peak into- Welcome to Shepherds Pass

# Chapter One

The average speed of a .22 caliber long rifle bullet is 1082 ft per second. It leaves the barrel of the gun at a temperature of more than 330 degrees Celsius. That is 626 degrees Fahrenheit. Then on impact with the human skull the bullet would penetrate the skull causing vibration, shock waves, and a burning trail of damage that would destroy all in its path. Commonly, the bullet would not have the same force after its deceleration upon passing through the cooler human body fluids, to escape the skull. Instead, the bullet would then proceed to ricochet and destroy randomly all it encountered. The result for the victim of the gunshot would be quite dead. This was the fate of many of the men in the alley in Shepherds Pass on the night it all began. There had been a light drizzle all evening, but that drizzle had not interrupted anything anyone had planned. It was welcomed. The warm Missouri evenings of May sometimes make people long for the relief of a brief respite.

In the 1800s a group of cattlemen involved in feuding with the local sheep herders had blocked the main path to water and grassland from the herds of sheep. The sheepherders accepted that they were outnumbered and outgunned and devised a secret pass that would allow them a back door into the watering holes and the plentiful grassland. The secret area became known later as Shepherds Pass. No one at that time needed to put Shepherds Pass on a map, lest war break out. When Highway 70 was built, an off-ramp was constructed to allow people access to the ragged, dilapidated town that had now sprung up, because the town offered two very vital things the area needed. First, was a gas station that carried diesel fuel for the trucks that moved down the highway all night long. And two if offered two all-night tow and auto repair shops. The repair shops were owned by the Dodd brothers Leo and Raymond. As the country grew and its needs changed so did the needs and tastes of the Dodd brothers. They became involved in gambling and prostitution and bootlegging during the twenties. The sins of man rained and caused the off-the-road Truckstop to grow into a small town.

At some point, the two Dodd brothers chose different paths. Leo Dodd married and started a family that fought hard to legitimize the existence of the family businesses. Leo Dodd's offspring sought education and philanthropy. Leo Dodd's children and their children would spend years after his death struggling to cleanse the family name.

Raymond Dodd and his children went the other path entirely. They believed in the ways of organized crime and sought just as hard to excel in their felonious endeavors as the Children of Leo did in education and goodwill. Due to a common beginning and the view from spectators from the outside the family they were destined to always be an overlap in the family's values and name.

# Chapter 2

Three men exited a shiny new rental car for a meeting with three other men. The first three men were led by a short stocky man chewing on a cigar that had long gone out. The stocky man carried a briefcase full of cash. You would not have to be told there was something of great value in the case, it was evident by the look on his face. The two men on his right and left were classic bodyguard types in shiny new suits. Their eyes focused straight ahead eyeing the group approaching. The group approaching looked like an almost mirror image of the first group. The short man in the center of the second group had no briefcase and his smile was even oilier than the simile of his counterpoint. "I hate Lawyers." The stocky man from the first group muttered almost to himself. Then he looked at the man on his right and then to the man on his left did I ever tell you guys about how much I hate lawyers." The first man's bodyguard grunted in harmony. "Once a lawyer screwed me so I ended up in the pen just so he could screw my wife at that time." his face contorted in a hideous remembrance. "I straighten that out when I got out, I only wish I could have killed them more than once." He chuckled in a deep baritone laugh. The meeting of the two groups was set for the alley behind a Chinese restaurant. The alleys in Shepherds Pass were remarkably clean. But the drizzle has started to loosen some other layers of ooze and sticky stuff found in alleys that no one is quite sure what it is or if they care to know. Shepherds Pass alleys were nothing like the alley in movies and on tv where there is an assortment of discards and derelicts, that seem to reach through the media you are watching and make you want a shower. With the mist and drizzle, the clean alley was even cleaner than usual. Light bounced off a red brick wall and laminated a spot where the corner of the building formed. Both groups of men walked toward the light. It was the natural place to conduct business on hand.

"This fucking blackmail." The speaker from the first group complained as the two groups converged under the light.

"It's greenmail and it's legal. Ask any lawyer."

"It's unethical as shit."

"So did you bring a priest or just the cash?"

There was a whistling undefinable sound not unlike a sworn of bees followed quickly by the dropping of two of the guards, one from each group. Another two guards fell and as the principals of the exchange turned to look toward the darkened area near the far corner, they had just enough time to make out two men emerging with the long barrel pistols. The two men emerged from the darkened corner toward the men under the light. The two last victims looked at each other in total disbelief. They had been so unprepared for a gun battle. And the direction from which the assault originated added insult to injury. In what seemed to be the final copulation the two last victims faced the shooters and did not even go for their guns, instead, they accepted the .22 long rifle bullets to their heads. And the damage was done; for now, they rested in the eternal sleep known as death.

# Don't miss out!

Visit the website below and you can sign up to receive emails whenever Alex Mitchell publishes a new book. There's no charge and no obligation.

https://books2read.com/r/B-A-UGUAB-DLZOC

**BOOKS 2 READ**

Connecting independent readers to independent writers.

# Also by Alex Mitchell

Welcome to Shepherds Pass
Revenge at Shepherds Pass
Treasure at Shepherds Pass
Welcome to Shepherds Pass
Man Among the Missing
Noreen Tyler
Robinhood at Shepherds Pass
That Which Makes Us Who We Are